# FROZEN BENEATH

*Brian Horeck*

---

Library and Archives Canada Cataloguing in Publication

Horeck, Brian

Frozen beneath

ISBN 978-0-9810434-0-1

---



Editing by Mary Taylor

Copy Editing by Katherine Coy

Front cover art by John Ellenberger,
Gerry Dunphy and Rob Lozier

Text design by Heidy Lawrance, WeMakeBooks.ca

12 11 10 09 08     2 3 4 5 6

Printed and bound in Canada

## ACKNOWLEDGEMENTS

James Rajotte: Forensics

Sergeant Buckle: Aurora Armoury

Sheguinandah Museum: Manitoulin Island

Chief Fidele Jokinen: Mississauga First Nation

Doug Olsen: Local trapper, Blind River

Sergeant Greg St-Aubin: Blind River OPP

Ben Vanags: Flight operations instructor

Bill Rajotte and Norm Pelland: "for you know!"

Ministry of Natural Resources: Blind River office

NORAD: North Bay, Ontario

# CHAPTER 1

In the early hours of a December morning a fierce blizzard had centred itself squarely over Northern Ontario, knocking down trees and stranding motorists in their cars on snow-blocked roads. Seated in a bright office, amongst a line of young technicians at the North American Aerospace Defense Center (NORAD) in North Bay, Ontario, Corporal John Gordon, a Canadian Tracking Technician watched his radarscope with coffee in hand.

Sergeant Kevin Stephenson, a U.S. Air Surveillance Technician, from southern Kentucky sat next to John, hands wrapped around his coffee mug. His five-o'clock shadow and scruffy dirty-blonde hair didn't detract from his good looks. Standing just over six feet with his muscular build made him a magnet for the women.

"I sure as hell hope they have our parking lot plowed out by morning," muttered Kevin in his thick southern Kentucky drawl.

"Huh! You're driving a 4 x 4 Jeep and you're paranoid over a few flakes of snow? And it's not like it's your first winter in Canada, eh?"

"Don't remind me. I still kick my ass for not taking that posting at Cheyenne Mountain."

John grinned as he rubbed the back of his shaved head. "Well, from the looks of the weather scope we'll be in snow up to our ass." John was just a tad shorter than Kevin. His athletic body came from playing sports and he loved the great outdoors.

Kevin and John were in their late twenties and had worked together for over a year at NORAD. They shared an apartment in town. Their co-workers were constantly entertained when they would razz each other with jokes of each other's government or country.

Kevin sighed. "Yeah, like I'm looking forward to another long cold Canadian winter."

"Maybe this winter we can take in some ice fishing on Lake Nipissing. I hear there is some great pickerel action out there."

The thought of a remote fishing trip excited Kevin. "Sounds good to me...and them there fish are called 'walleye', not 'pickerel'."

John escalated his voice for the other technicians to overhear. "No Kevin. You Americans call them walleyes. We Canadians call them pickerel."

Kevin scoffed. "Well then John, I would suggest that you write to the editor of *Outdoor Canada* magazine and chew his ass off over this month's article on 'Ultimate Ice Fishing for Whitefish and Walleye'. It's sitting on the table in the Officer's Mess. And that reminds me...you still owe me for an all-expense paid ice fishing weekend from last year's Super Bowl bet."

John knew that Kevin had him and he had to come clean in front of the other technicians. "OK, you made me eat crow on the walleye bullshit." He high-fived Kevin. "And I'll come clean on that ice fishing trip this winter. It should be quite the laugh taking a Southerner from Kentucky ice fishing when the only ice a hillbilly ever saw was probably in their whiskey."

Suddenly, out of the blue, an image appeared on John's radarscope. Unlike most tracks this one was coming in from outer space.

"I have incoming from up yonder," said John, mocking Kevin's Kentucky accent.

"Hell we do," agreed Kevin, carefully scanning John's radarscope. The ball was now in Kevin's court, being Head Surveillance Technician. His protocol for the next few seconds was to make a quick evaluation of the object that was entering into Canadian airspace. He took in factors such as location, speed and trajectory. No other commercial or private flights were close to that location. NORAD had not received a Mayday alarm. Based on all the data and factors, Kevin felt that there was no reason to scramble fighter aircraft to intercept. He quickly made the decision to declare it bad data, thus stopping the actual flow of information to the Air Defense Squadron. Kevin took a deep breath and laid a hand on John's shoulder. "Well John, I'd have to say that by its speed and trajectory and point of entry that it has to be a meteor. I just declared it bad data. Hell, by the time we alert them air jockeys that space shit would have already crashed."

John was not really sure he understood Kevin through his accent. He turned to face Kevin. "I'm sorry Kev, did you say space ship?"

"No you smart ass. I said space *shit*."

John lowered his voice so as not to attract attention from other technicians. "Hell, you can call it anything you want. You're the big cheese."

Kevin's face tightened. "Are you questioning my call on the validity of that track?"

"Not at all, that sucker is the size of a school bus and I tracked it to where it crashed. It's just north of a town called Blind River."

"Blind River? Where in the hell is that? Next to Deaf Lake?"

"No" chuckled John. "It's located northwest between Sudbury and Sault Ste. Marie, on the Trans-Canada Highway. It crashed along the north end of a Lake called Matinenda. Its UTM coordinates are Zone 17, E352584 and N5140588."

Kevin nodded. "Good show. Now get onto Google Earth to see if there are any landmarks close by that meteor crash site. I'll get them to take some satellite aerials on the day shift provided it's not buried by this snowfall."

"Well how about that," said John intrigued, looking at a monitor. "It looks like it's just inland a little on the north end of Lake Matinenda, to the east of Shamas Bay. The closest private lots to that meteor are in the far end of the bay. According to this, there are no roads into them but there is a hydro and gas pipeline, a mile due north."

"No shit...good thing it didn't crash there. It's highly unlikely we'll be getting a call from the OPP then. I'm sure no one would have seen it crash in this storm, at this hour!"

"You're probably right."

Kevin grabbed John's coffee mug. "I'll get us a fresh refill."

Minutes later Kevin picked up a printout of the crash site from John's desk and set his coffee down.

John's eyes were glued to his radarscope. "Interesting isn't it?" asked John, knowing Kevin was reviewing the printout.

"Yes, but not as interesting as this..." Kevin pulled a rolled up newspaper from under his arm and unrolled it in front of John. "It's yesterday's *Globe and Mail.* I found it in the mess hall."

Kevin waited patiently as John scanned the story headline.

"Hmmm. 'Space Rocks in Eastern Manitoba, Amateur Geologist Tracks down Meteorite Hot Spot.' John looked up at Kevin while taking a sip of coffee. "Well holy shit, talk about déjà vu."

Kevin chuckled. "No shit! Those two small meteorites you see that man holding were found in an area east of Winnipeg near the boundary of Ontario. Hey, now that I say that, I can remember when I was a young'un back in Walton when a local farmer found one of them there meteorites in his cornfield. They used to say that some government people gave him some big bucks for that there thing."

John's fingers began to tap on his desk. Kevin could see that he was deep in thought. John slowly swiveled his chair around and pulled the crash printout from Kevin's hand and glanced over it one more time. "Are you thinking what I'm thinking?

Because we're both off for the first ten days in January so what do "ya'll" say we plan for a little ice fishing and rock hunting trip in Blind River?"

"You're on," said Kevin, holding up his coffee mug to toast. "To our fishing trip in Blind River!"

# CHAPTER 2

Thursday December 14th. Four days after China used a ballistic missile to destroy one of their own obsolete satellites, two elderly gray haired men, US Vice President Scotty Bornman, and soon to be retired US Air Force General Mike Mackwood, stood side-by-side on the tarmac alongside an army motorcade at Area #51, the US Air force top-secret fighter jet testing grounds near Nevada, known to some as "*Dreamland.*" Each is looking skyward through binoculars at a black V-shaped fighter jet trailing a long purplish streak.

"Yes Scotty. What you are witnessing today is history. Project Arrowhead. The world's first space plane," said the General with a content smile.

"You mean the top of the President's Christmas wish list," replied the Vice President, still following the jet through his field glasses.

"Right now in our atmosphere it's taking in air through its skin like our space shuttle but once it enters outer space it will switch over to hydro carbon fuel, allowing it to cruise at mach 25."

The Vice President lowered his binoculars and glanced at the General. "Did you say mach 25?"

"Yes Scotty. Mach 25," replied Mike still looking up through his field glasses. "The same speed in which our space shuttle re-enters our atmosphere...and as a matter of fact, Arrowhead's belly has a heat shield similar to the space shuttle."

"Who's the test pilot?"

"No one. Arrowhead is a pilotless craft with a computer-operated robot. With its unique hydraulics drive system we can program and guide it by our operational satellite."

The Vice President's eyes narrowed. "You don't mean the one we launched for the Star Wars Project?"

"That's the one," replied Mike with a mischievous smile. "And with Arrowhead's state-of-the-art weaponry it can take out up to twelve targets at once plus its wings fold inwardly to fit into that white transport parked over there. So it can be hidden and transported out of view of spy satellites."

The Vice President, impressed by all this new technology, nodded with a content frown at Mike, then returned his binoculars to his eyes. "So what exactly did you mean by targets?"

Mike was slow to respond. "Oh, you know...terrorists...warheads...or enemy spy satellites." Mike nudged Scotty. "You know, taking them out in outer space has its advantages." Mike knew full well that he tickled the Vice President's ears.

The sound of someone clearing his throat could be heard from behind them. "Now gentlemen, if I can have your attention for just a minute."

Scotty and Mike turned around to face a small man wearing a white lab jacket with a laptop computer opened up on a small table beside him. "Good morning, I'm Ted Foxwell," he said with a warm smile as he shook their hands. "Sent here from Kennedy Space Center's Research and Development to help conduct this test with you two."

Scotty and Mike watched him closely as he reached down and pushed a button on the keyboard. An image of a white satellite with a USA flag insignia flashed on the monitor.

Ted looked up at them. "This gentlemen, is our target for today's test."

The thought of using a US multi-million-dollar satellite for a target baffled both men. Bornman and Mackwood locked eyes, both at a loss for words.

"Oh, don't worry men," chuckled Ted. "It's an obsolete weather satellite. What you see appearing just to the left on the monitor now is Arrowhead," he continued, looking back at the Vice President. "It's already been programmed to take it out...so, sir...if you would like to do the honours, just push '*Enter*' on the keyboard and observe."

Slowly the Vice President looked back at the General. From the look on Scotty's face the General could sense his hesitation.

Mackwood patted Scotty's shoulder. "Go ahead, sir. You will save taxpayers the cost of recovering it."

"Well, I suppose you're right," said Scotty as he reached out and pushed '*Enter*'.

That instant the satellite disintegrated into a bright orange cloud and disappeared from view.

All three men looked to the sky in silence. No trace of what they had just witnessed remained.

"Whoa! Unbelievable!" exclaimed Scotty. "I'm betting that one of China's spy satellites caught that show. They should be calling the Pentagon right about now. Mike, I'm sure that the President will be very, very happy with his Christmas gift."

# CHAPTER 3

On a cold, late afternoon, in early January, two men in their early fifties ventured out across the ice-covered surface of Lake Matinenda through a blizzard. Each wore a two-way radio communicator under his helmet.

J.P. Cyr, a short and stocky French Canadian, led the way on his long track snowmobile, towing a large, black, casket-like sleigh. Following closely on his Tracked ATV was J.P.'s best friend, Greg Kawalski, who stood six foot two, with a large muscular frame. Because of their noticeable size difference they were referred to as "the odd couple" or "the big *Polak* and little Frenchman."

They were young at heart with a good sense of humour. Rain, sleet or snow would never be a reason for them to renege on a fishing or hunting trip. They had endured the savage splendor of this terrain for years.

The track of J.P.'s snowmobile kicked up a stinging spray of granulated snow that caked onto Greg's windshield, forcing him to peer over it. Greg transmitted to J.P., "I'm sorry but you're *gonna* have to slow down. I'm having trouble following with all that shit you're throwing up at me."

"OK, den Greg. If dat will help you dere," replied J.P. over his radio in his thick French Canadian accent as he eased off on his throttle, reducing his speed by 10 mph.

"OK, J.P. That should do it for now."

The snowfall grew heavier by the minute as they approached the long, narrow cove that passed between an island and the mainland, known to locals as Graveyard Narrows, named for the number of snowmobilers and ice-fishermen who had drowned there over the years. A swift current ran through the deep, narrow channel preventing ice from freezing thick enough to support a man or snowmobile. The key to getting through this treacherous channel was to travel at a high speed to defy gravity while hugging the steep, rocky shoreline to the left.

The large sled that J.P. was towing could hinder the performance of his snowmobile and that played on Greg's mind. "Well J.P., what do you think?"

J.P. wasn't quick to respond. He was concentrating on the ice and current patterns ahead of them. "I tink we should give her shit dere."

"OK then. Lets give'r. I'll be right on your ass."

J.P. pinned down his throttle tight to the handlebar, accelerating his snowmobile into high gear, kicking up a high and wide rooster tail of snow that obstructed Greg's view. He noticed a small opening in the ice about twenty yards ahead of them. "Open hole ahead," he yelled into his microphone, steering his snowmobile slightly to the left, his knees squeezing the seat like a vice, he knew that the slightest miscalculation in the narrow channel would mean certain death.

As J.P. approached the opening in the ice, he concentrated on keeping his snowmobile as tight to the steep, rocky shoreline as possible. Glancing to his right he couldn't help but notice the dark open hellhole waiting to consume its next contestant. He felt a sudden hard jolt from the back of his snowmobile that startled him. The thought of Greg rear-ending him on thin ice was his worst nightmare. Looking down at his mirror he realized that it was the swaying motion of the sleigh he was towing that sideswiped against the rocky shoreline. Greg's headlight in his mirror was confirmation that they had made it through the gates of hell.

"Holy shit," shouted Greg over J.P.'s radio. "Your fuckin' sleigh almost cost me my life. I couldn't see a fuckin' thing from all the slush that you threw back at me."

A number of comebacks came to J.P.'s mind as he drove on but he chose silence, letting Greg cool off.

Although treacherous, Graveyard Narrows had sheltered them from the wind. As they came out in the open, it was a whole new perspective, with a combination of gusting winds and heavier snowfall causing whiteout conditions.

Greg was doing his best to keep J.P. in sight when, out of the blue, J.P. veered his snowmobile sharply to the right and cut his speed down to a crawl, forcing Greg to hit his brakes to prevent a rear-end collision. Greg was perturbed by J.P.'s unexpected maneuver, it had caught him by surprise.

This time it was Greg's turn to bite his tongue. He knew J.P. would have good reason for the stunt and taking them off course.

Suddenly, J.P. hunched his small body forward and stood up on his chassis runner boards, elevating himself above his windshield. He stared intensely into the heavy snowfall while his snowmobile crawled forward.

Greg's mind swirled. *Could it be a pack of timber wolves that caught J.P.'s eyes*, he wondered, as he too looked intensely in the same northerly direction. At times Greg could faintly make out a dark distant tree line across the lake, but saw nothing of whatever had alarmed his buddy.

J.P. brought his snowmobile to a halt as Greg pulled up and parked alongside him.

"So what in the hell was it that almost got your ass run over?"

J.P. turned his helmet to make eye contact. "I don't know," he replied sternly.

Greg shook his head. "Whatever it was got you interested enough to take us off course."

J.P. knew from Greg's harsh comment he would have to do better than that. He locked eyes with Greg. "OK den...it was someting big and dark."

Greg knew that despite J.P.'s age, his eyes were the same keen and sharp ones that had proved themselves on numerous hunting trips. Those eyes stared back at him now. He knew he had to let J.P. have the benefit of the doubt. Greg took a deep breath. "OK then, just bear with me for a minute." Greg slid off one of his big mitts and reached deep into his parka pocket, pulling out a small yellow plastic object.

"Holy shit Greg. Is dat one of dem dere tings dat shows you where you are?"

"Yes. It's a GPS."

"Well, I tink Santa was pretty damn good to you dis year."

"No J.P. This was *my* treat." Greg held it out so J.P. could see it up close. "I just keyed up this part of the lake from the Graveyard Narrows to here. I logged the whole lake into the GPS so we could drive through shit like this. I even logged in to where we will be putting our fishing hut this year. It should be right across from that shore, just to the right of Shamas Bay." He pointed.

"Well, I would have to say dats a pretty smart Polak den," said J.P.

"No J.P. If I were so smart I wouldn't have let a Frenchman lead to begin with," laughed Greg.

"Maudit Polak!" replied J.P.

"OK J.P. This is the plan." Greg held out his GPS for J.P. to view. "It will lead us due north, just to the right of Shamas Bay. That did seem to be where you saw that big dark thing and it's also close to where we want to put our fishing shack."

"You mean where we caught all dem nice trout last March?"

"That's right...and our camp is only ten minutes west of there. I don't want to waste too much time on this wild goose chase. I'd like to be settled in before dark."

"OK den. It's my turn to follow."

"You mean to eat snow!" Greg pinned down on his throttle, throwing up a large rooster tail of slush at J.P., covering him from head to toe.

"Maudit Polak!" hollered J.P. into the radio.

Glancing into his mirror he saw J.P. cleaning the slush off his helmet visor. "Well now, isn't payback a bitch," he chuckled.

Greg and J.P. weren't two minutes further up the lake when Greg's eyes caught a faint silhouette of a dark structure rising up from the barren lake. "Holy shit! I can see something straight ahead."

"I see it too," replied J.P. with relief. He wasn't seeing things after all.

They were both bewildered as they approached the mysterious object. Every second seemed like a minute as the dark structure became more visible.

"Fuuuck," Greg scowled, his voice intensifying. "Who in the hell put that here?"

"Tabarnak!" shouted J.P. He too was irked after realizing it was a fishing hut that had attracted them. For years no one but them had set up a fishing hut this far north on the lake.

Greg drove his ATV up close to the hut and slowly circled around, examining every inch of the mysterious, new shanty and then parked his ATV on the south side of the hut, which sheltered them from the storm.

J.P. parked his snowmobile beside Greg. "Well Greg...what do you tink?"

"I don't know who in the hell it could belong to. No one at this end of the lake ever uses their camp in the winter, or ice fishes for that matter. We can't even see where they towed it from because of the fresh snowfall."

"Well, I know one ting for sure, me..."

"And what's that?" Greg asked.

"Dere is no fuckin way dat dey brought dat dere shack through the Graveyard Narrows."

Greg slowly nodded. "You're absolutely right. There is no way in hell that thin ice could support this mother."

Suddenly, a loud, screeching noise came over their communicators. "Yikes!" shouted Greg, shaking off his mitt to turn off his communicator switch as J.P. did the same. "Son of a bitch. What in the hell!" Greg unstrapped his helmet and yanked it off. "Damn it. That's all we need...for these things to act up on the first day we use 'em."

"Dat was a crazy haywire sound to me," said J.P., checking his communicator.

Greg put just his earphones on and turned them back on. "I'll try her again." A loud shrilling noise echoed out of the earphones. "That's bullshit!" He yanked them back off his head. "They're under warranty but we're here for two weeks. Just my luck."

J.P. handed his set to Greg. "We don't need dat bullshit stuff anyway."

Greg pulled out his GPS and turned it on. "Might as well check this out. Well, son of a bitch. Not this too!" He rolled his eyes back, disgusted. "Is this a *Murphy* day?"

"What do you mean by '*Murphy dey*'?" asked J.P.

"Oh, it's just a theory that some guy by the name of Murphy dreamed up. He said that if anything could go wrong, chances are, it will go wrong. They call it *Murphy's Law*. See what I mean?" He showed J.P. the GPS screen. The screen was filled with squiggly lines.

"Well, I'm sorry Greg but I don't know nottin' about dat bullshit me."

Greg put his helmet back on and climbed up on his ATV. "You know, you're right J.P. It's bullshit. And after all this bullshit I just want to get to the camp, light the stove and have myself a shot."

J.P. started up his snowmobile. "I'm for dat, me."

Greg started his ATV. "We'll just follow the tree line back like old times." While driving off, Greg glanced into his mirror back at the fishing hut. There was something mysterious about it that nagged his thoughts.

# CHAPTER 4

That same day, back in North Bay, John sat at his kitchen table with a beer in hand, gazing at the monitor of a laptop computer. A constant sound of gears turning echoed throughout the small kitchen. Kevin sat across the table, reeling in new fishing line from a plastic spool that lay on the kitchen floor.

"This is crazy. I just googled '*meteorite*'. I got '*meteorites for sale*'.... '*Deal with Canadians and save*'... '*ebay.ca*' ...and '*save through ebay*'."

"You're shitting me," said Kevin.

"No shit, there has to be at least a dozen sites that buy and sell meteorites."

"I hope ours is worth something." Kevin smiled contentedly.

"Now this is interesting," continued John. "There are three broad categories. '*Stony*' meteorites are rocks mainly composed of silicate minerals, '*Iron*' meteorites are largely composed of metallic iron-nickel, and '*Stony-Iron*' meteorites contain both metallic and rocky material."

Kevin stopped reeling. "Well my money is on the iron-nickel meteorite. Ninety percent nickel and ten percent iron."

"Now that's wishful thinking," said John.

Kevin held his fishing reel up to John. "Do you figger I have enough line on her?"

"Oh yeah..." John reached over from his chair to open the fridge door.

Kevin cut the excess line from the rod tip. "It's sure gonna be great to have a little 'R and R."

"Oh yeah... I did get back to that sexy-voice from the Lodge."

"You mean Lori?" asked Kevin.

"Yes.... Lori. I hope she looks as good as she sounds. Apparently you can use your laptop there but it's not high-speed."

"Oh well...as long as I can e-mail my mother."

"It's nice you keep in touch with her."

"Well, at fifty-five she's doing good. She wants me to e-mail her a picture of my first fish I catch through the ice."

"I'd gladly let you hold up one of mine for the photo," chuckled John.

"So, have you got all our stops in Blind River figured out?" asked Kevin.

"You tell me." John pushed some keys on the laptop then turned it around for Kevin to see. "Thanks to their Chamber of Commerce website all of our shopping is made easy."

Kevin checked out the town map and local businesses that John had highlighted.

"First stop, beer, right there on the Trans-Canada Highway, then over next to that, Value Mart grocery store for our munchies, then turn right at the Royal Bank onto Woodward Avenue, down to Mustang's Grill or Iron Horse Tavern for a beer and burger break, then across the street to the liquor store for hot toddy mix, then drive three minutes to the right to U-Rentals Bait and Tackle to pick up snowmobile rentals and minnows. From there it's only 20 minutes north to the Lodge."

"I'd say you plotted a pretty good course to follow," said Kevin.

"So how did your shopping go at the Armories this morning?" asked John.

"Oh, I got us some army winter whites with boots, mitts and balaclavas... snowshoes, thermal tent and arctic sleeping bags... heaters, shovels, mess kit, first aid kit, Army landmine scanner and night vision goggles and a surprise."

John sat higher in his chair. "A landmine scanner *and* night vision goggles?"

"Hell yeah...It will make it a hell of a lot easier to locate that meteor under all that snow."

"Hmmm...I guess that makes sense. But night vision goggles?"

"Just in case we run into too many people around that area during the day we'll have an alternative. And besides, we can always use them for night fishing."

John took a swig from his bottle. "Ha! I would say that for a redneck hillbilly you surprise me at times."

# CHAPTER 5

After following the contour of the shoreline for some time Greg turned his ATV hard to the right, into a long, narrow inlet. A thick growth of tall, snow-covered pine trees standing along its steep, rocky banks made for a picturesque view. It reminded Greg of all those *Hallmark* Christmas cards he'd left on his mantle at home.

Greg and J.P. were now sheltered from the high winds as they advanced inwardly. They soon reached the end of the inlet. Just ahead, Greg's cottage began to appear through the thick snowfall. It was a large log cabin that had been passed down from his father. It sat nestled up high on a ridge amongst the huge, white pines. Winter or summer, it was a place Greg went to get away from his day-to-day activities, to focus his thoughts and just be one with nature.

A steep, wide trail led Greg and J.P. up to the cottage. They parked their machines in front of a long, covered verandah. They had just taken off their helmets when they heard a distant sound of a snowmobile approaching. Greg looked over at J.P. "I think we're getting company."

"I don't know dat ski-doo," said J.P. as they watched it drive off the lake.

"Well, it's not a conservation officer. They always pair up with an OPP officer," said Greg.

A new, silver-gray snowmobile pulled up and parked alongside J.P.'s cargo sleigh. Greg and J.P. stood patiently, wondering who this mysterious person was: showing up at the north end of the lake, through a snowstorm, late in the afternoon. *Could this person be lost*?

"I heard that the twins were on the lake," said a tall, slender, young man as he lifted his helmet visor and stood up from his snowmobile.

"Well I'll be a son of a bitch. Darren, how in the hell are ya?" asked Greg with a cheerful smile, reaching his hand out to greet their young visitor. Darren's father and mother had been good friends of Greg and J.P. They had died two years ago in a tragic automotive accident.

Greg frowned and nodded his head as he admired Darren's new snowmobile with its long track and sleek look. "Hmmmm. Nice sled."

"Thanks Greg," said Darren as he stared down at the tracks on Greg's ATV. So…how does your bike handle with those tracks on her?

"It's not as fast as a snowmobile but it'll go anywhere."

I thought that was your truck and trailer parked at the boat launch," said Darren. I followed your tracks up to the north end of Graveyard Narrows till I lost them, then I picked them up again half-way across the north end. What's up with that?"

Both Greg and J.P. smiled realizing how confusing the tracks, or lack thereof, have been for Darren. "Oh *ya*, it's a good story all right," said Greg while unfastening a bungee cord off J.P.'s sled.

Darren smiled. "A 'good story', like setting a few night lines?"

"No, no, nothing like that. But you're close. Help us get settled in and you can hear our interesting story over a beer," said Greg as he lifted a large duffel bag out from the sled. He glanced back at J.P. as he kicked snow off the steps. "Why don't you take the ice auger down to the lake and cut us a hole for water while I get the fire started?"

Within an hour, the sound of the crackling fire and the radiant heat being thrown from the old wood stove warmed the rustic cabin, as the boys settled around the kitchen table reminiscing over cold beers.

"Well Darren, I'm still pissed off at the old fart for not selling the Lodge to you after accepting your offer," said Greg leaning back in his chair.

"Don't be," said Darren. "It turned out to be some legal bullshit with his sister back in Ohio that put a stop to the sale."

"Yes, but it must have cost you for your lawyer," said Greg.

"Sure it did," nodded Darren, "but old Charley agreed on paper that when he sells it I will have first dibs on it at that same price. So the insurance money I inherited from my parents is collecting interest. Meantime, I got an apartment upstairs at the Riverside Hotel and I'm bartending downstairs for Big Bob and his brother. I even finished a course in Hotel and Restaurant Management at Canador College in North Bay. So the so-called waiting game is just making me stronger."

Greg nodded. "I'm really impressed. Most kids your age would only be interested in beer, parties, and pussy. You got your shit together. Ben and Linda would be very proud of you. Here's to Ben and Linda and a great son," said Greg, holding up his beer to toast. "Oh shit, I almost forgot to turn on my cell phone!" Greg stood and strode to his bedroom.

Greg returned seconds later with a black-bag cell phone in one hand and a travel brochure in the other. He tossed the brochure on top of the table next to Darren as he plugged the cell phone into a car battery which stood on the kitchen counter. "Check it out. Our wives are working on their tans in Jamaica while we're fishing our asses off."

"I was about to ask you guys where the girls were," said Darren as he picked up the brochure.

"Yeah, it's hard to beat this," said Greg looking out the window at the large snow-flakes.

Darren nodded. "Yeah, but a nude beach with all that eye candy sounds a little more inviting!"

"Nude beach?"

Darren turned the brochure for Greg to see. "It says here that swimsuits are optional."

Greg scoffed. "Just wait till Sherry gets home!"

Darren grinned. "You know what white women say about black men?"

Greg pointed at Darren. "Don't go there!"

"Well, I know one ting for sure is dat beer dere has vitamin pee and I have to get rid of some of dat, me," said J.P. as he put his boots on and stomped out the door. A few minutes later he returned from outside. "Did you bring in the minnows Greg?"

"No. Did you Darren?" asked Greg.

Darren lowered the brochure and shook his head.

Greg scratched his head. "Well, we packed everything from the truck."

"I remember dat dere too," replied J.P.

"Oh shit," said Greg. "Don't tell me we forgot them back in Blind River at U-Rental. We paid for them with all those new jigs and gas but I remember putting the two plastic bags into that small blue and white cooler."

J.P. shook his head with a disgusted look. "Merde! I remember now putting dat cooler down outside at the gas pump."

"That's no problem," said Darren. "I'm sure they will set them aside for you. I'll pick them up on my way back in a couple of days."

"I'd appreciate that," said Greg. "And you're welcome to join us. We'll have our shack parked to the right side of Shamas Bay next to that mystery one."

"Mystery one?" asked Darren. "You mean a fishing hut?"

Greg nodded. "Yes, it's a new one. That's the story we wanted to tell you earlier. J.P. first noticed something dark this side of Graveyard Narrows. That's what led us off course earlier."

Darren shrugged. "I can't imagine how they got it there. There's no *freakin* way it could have been towed through Graveyard

Narrows. I can't think of anyone who would be fishing at this end."

Greg took a swig from his beer. "We thought the exact same thing. And oddly enough, it's the same *freakin* spot where we caught those nice lake trout last March."

Darren sympathized with Greg. "Fuck it. Put your shack up close to theirs. They can't own water."

Greg gave them a mysterious grin. "I *knew* there was something different about that shack! He reached up to a shelf, turning on the radio.

"And what was dat?" asked J.P.

"No registration numbers," replied Greg as an old hit song from Shania Twain, '*That Don't Impress Me Much*' played over a local FM channel.

"I'll ask around at the Riverside tomorrow. Doug Olson might drop in if he's not trapping," said Darren.

"Well, if you want to know anything about Blind River, that's the place," chuckled Greg.

Suddenly the song on the radio was overtaken by a low, eerie, moaning-like sound. It sounded like low cords strummed on a bass fiddle.

"That don't impress me much either," mocked Greg as he reached up to the radio's tuning knob.

"Oh, what's the matter Greg? You don't like the change in Shania's voice?" laughed Darren.

"No. She sounds like a cow moose in heat," said Greg as he stood from his chair, trying to tune the channel.

Bewildered, Darren and J.P. watched as Greg tried tuning in to another channel but the strange, spooky sound dominated even between channels.

"That's bullshit," said Greg as he set the radio on the table. "I just wanted to know the forecast for tomorrow. I can't even get CBC."

"Dat's the same bullshit dat happened over at dat shack," said J.P.

Greg nodded. "You're right. That's the same tone that came over our communicators."

"You're kidding," said Darren.

"No shit," said Greg as he turned off the radio and placed it back on the shelf. "And come to think of it, my new GPS wouldn't even function."

Darren reached into his pocket and pulled out his own GPS. "It works off a satellite Greg, I can't see why they'd be connected." Darren smiled as he pushed the '*ON*' button. Greg and J.P. gazed down at the GPS. Scrambled lines appeared on the monitor. Darren leaned toward his GPS and drew in his breath. "This is bullshit!"

"I agree," said Greg opening his hands on the table. "Just a minute ago the radio was working fine and then that freak sound."

"Whoa, whoa, *tabarnak*!" said J.P. pointing down at the GPS. A clear dotted image of Darren's route to Greg's cottage appeared on the monitor.

"Well I'll be a son of a bitch," said Greg as he reached for his radio. To their surprise it worked well, on every channel. "Now I'll get the forecast," he said as he took a swig from his beer bottle.

Darren stood up and reached for his coat. "I'll bet it's that new cell tower at Lake

Lauzon that is causing all this shit. But then again, it wouldn't interfere with a GPS."

Greg suddenly uncomfortable with Darren's plan to leave, spoke up. "So what's your hurry Darren? I was just going to put one of Sherry's deep-dish lasagnas in the oven...and you know we have an extra room. Doesn't look like the snow has let up and it's getting dark."

"Ah, thanks, but I promised Lori that I would play a couple of games of pool at the Lodge with her before heading back to Blind River. Plus I have to open the Riverside for Big Bob tomorrow."

Greg glanced down at his watch and realized Darren would make it before dark. "OK but do me a favour and say 'hi' to Bob and Derek at the Riverside."

"Sure thing Greg. And keep me a leftover piece of Sherry's lasagna for the ice hut when I bring you back your minnows," said Darren as he pulled on the rest of his outdoor gear. "I'll call you, and—hey, thanks for the beer."

As the door closed behind Darren, Greg and J.P. looked at each other over their beers in the suddenly silent cottage. Within a minute they could hear the sound of Darren's snowmobile starting. Greg stared down at his beer bottle as he scratched on the label with his thumbnails. "Yep. He's a good young man. I just hope old Charley doesn't screw him on the sale of that Lodge."

# CHAPTER 6

Another bone-chilling morning in North Bay greeted John and Kevin in their apartment parking lot. Both were dressed in full army winter whites and they shuffled their duffle bags and gear as they packed Kevin's Jeep Cherokee. White clouds rose up from their mouths as they exhaled into the frigid air.

John pulled out a wolf fur hat from one of his bags and covered his chilled head.

"So that's what you Canadians call a 'block heater'. Or should I just call you the 'mad trapper'?" smirked Kevin. He too could no longer expose his bare head to the bitter cold and pulled out some kind of fur hat. Unlike John's, Kevin's hat bore the face of a small animal with pointy ears, nose and black beady eyes.

John stared at Kevin with an uncertain expression. "Isn't Groundhog Day next month or were you hoping to see your shadow?"

"Smart ass," replied Kevin as he pulled a thick, ringed bushy tail out from under the hat and let it dangle from behind. "Hell boy. Haven't ya'll ever seen a coonskin hat before?" Kevin's hat complemented his Kentucky accent.

John did his best not to break out in laughter. "Now if you were wearing a buckskin jacket I'd call you Daniel Boone."

Kevin smirked. "No, I'm sorry John…but you were thinking of Davy Crockett."

John's eyes narrowed. "Are you sure?"

"Remember the Alamo. John Wayne played Davy Crockett wearing a coonskin hat. He was a colonel from Tennessee." Kevin handed John his laptop case. "I want this in the front with us. I downloaded something that you just *have* to see."

The Jeep was about to exit the parking lot when John raised his index finger. "Oh shit. Stop for a *sec*. I almost forgot."

Kevin stopped the Jeep as John jumped out and ran to his car. Kevin watched John open his trunk then pull out a long wooden pole that had a sharp metal chisel tip at one end. Kevin had never seen anything like it before. He took a closer look as John loaded it into the Jeep. "So you plan on harpooning seals with that thing?" he asked as they exited the parking lot.

John smiled. "Hell no. Why would I want to piss off Pamela Anderson? That's for snow snakes."

Kevin's eyes widened. "Snow snakes. Are you shitting me?"

# CHAPTER 7

The aroma of freshly perked coffee lingered in the air as Greg and J.P. enjoyed a hearty breakfast in the warm log camp. They looked out through the picture window. Beams of sunlight filtered through the fresh, white snow. Hanging from pine branches in the clear, still air, blue jays took their turns grabbing whole peanuts off the window ledge as a song played on the radio.

"Oh, dere comes dat big one again for more," said J.P. as he folded his toast around a breakfast sausage then rubbed it into the remaining egg yolk on his plate.

"Yeah…He's probably storing them up in some tree for later," said Greg sipping his coffee.

The song ended on the radio.

*"Welcome to Moose FM news. Moose FM would like to apologize to all its listeners throughout its broadcast region for interruptions that occurred from early yesterday morning to the late hours last night. The station has found out that this same interference has also happened on other FM and AM stations in the area as well as cell phones. Our technicians are looking..."*

Just then, the same deep eerie sound came back over the radio.

"Well, son of a bitch," said Greg as he reached up from his chair and turned the radio off. "So that explains why the girls didn't get through on the phone last night and the deejay said that this shit was happening on all the other stations in this broadcast area, even cell phones. That can't be... because they have their own towers."

J.P. reached over with the coffee pot to top off Greg's mug. "Well den, what about dat GPS dat you and Darren have?"

Greg heaved a sigh while gazing into his coffee. "This doesn't make any sense... because GPS operate only off of satellites."

## CHAPTER 8

Heading west on the Trans-Canada Highway for over an hour, John reviewed some images that Kevin had downloaded the night before.

"Holy shit, Kevin. This image is really incredible. That Chinese ballistic missile really made a monkey out of that satellite."

Kevin glanced over at John with a modest smile. "Yep. It was one of their old weather satellites. That footage was taken from one of our satellites."

"So what in the hell do you think they're trying to prove?" asked John as he took a sip of his Tim Horton's coffee.

"Ah, it's probably China and Russia's way of inviting us to the negotiation table to talk about a space treaty deal. That destruction took place on the twelfth of

December. Now if you thought that image was incredible, it only gets better."

John raised his brows. "Better?"

Kevin nodded. "Big time."

"The next footage was taken from one of NASA's satellites on the fourteenth, just two days later."

John clicked on to the next video. It was a space shot of big blue planet earth with a satellite orbiting in front. A dark, V-shaped object suddenly appeared, trailing a long purplish streak. John watched in amazement as it headed right into the path of the satellite. A reddish beam of light flashed from the craft toward the satellite. Instantly the satellite scattered into a cloud of dust.

John had never witnessed an attack of such destruction. He just sat there, bewildered.

Kevin knew this was going to take John by surprise. "That image was taken from NASA's 'earth disruption system'."

John shook his head. "Houston, we have a problem," he mumbled. "I'm sorry Kevin but I'm just astounded over this. For a second I thought I was watching a sci-fi movie or something."

Kevin laughed. "Well, you're part right. It's the US military testing an advanced classified aircraft. A part of the Star Wars program."

John paused. "So what makes you think it's a US aircraft?"

"Because it was an old U.S. weather satellite that was taken out."

John nodded. "Oh, OK. It's all making sense to me now. The big boys are having a pissing contest. So how in the hell did you obtain this?"

"From one of my buddies at the Air Defence Sector, in Cheyenne Mountain. Hell John, I reckon by the time we get back to the base we're gonna have briefings coming out our *wing-wangs*."

Later that morning John and Kevin visited the Big Nickel, a popular tourist attraction in the city of Sudbury. A huge nickel replica sat high on a pedestal, symbolizing the wealth that the city of Sudbury had contributed to the Canadian economy through nickel production. The history of geology and mining of the area could be learned here.

John pressed on the shutter button of his digital camera that rested on the hood of the Jeep. Kevin stood patiently in front of the Big Nickel as John ran toward him.

"OK, now...give a big smile for mom back home!" said John as he put his arm around Kevin's shoulder. "This picture will be called the 'meteor capital of the world'."

Kevin squinted. "I thought Sudbury was called the *nickel* capital of the world."

John nodded in agreement. "Yes, but scientists claim that it was a giant meteor that crashed and left this rich nickel deposit."

A smile grew on Kevin's face as he turned around to take a closer look at the Big Nickel. "Hell it would be sure nice if our meteor has at least half of that amount of nickel."

# CHAPTER 9

A picturesque winter morning on the lake —the storm of the evening before had cleared out in the early hours, leaving behind trees blanketed in snow and a brilliant blue sky. J.P. exited from the inlet, cruising slowly on his snowmobile. Greg followed close behind on his ATV, towing a large ice fishing shanty. Minutes later J.P. brought his snowmobile down to a crawl, swiveling his head from side to side, trying to line up landmarks on opposite shorelines, making sure that their fishing hut would be parked in just the right spot. Suddenly he brought his sled to a halt and killed the engine. Greg pulled up alongside, squinting across at the mystery hut parked less than 40 yards away.

Greg nodded briefly. "We should be meeting them by the weekend. Are you sure this is the right spot?" he asked as he put on a beaver pelt hat.

J.P. dismounted from his sled and kicked the snow to clear a small spot on the lake's surface. "Now, how about dat...my *X* is still here from last year."

Greg laughed and shook his head. "Now how could I argue with that?" He opened a thermos and filled two thermal coffee mugs.

J.P. finished unhitching the fishing hut from the ATV as Greg handed him a mug.

Greg lifted his mug out toward J.P., "Here's to a great winter's fishing!"

"I'll toast to dat, me. Cha-ching, tabarnak!" He took a sip from his mug and then looked at Greg. "Dat's funny, your coffee dere always tastes a little better den Tim Horton's."

"Maybe because they skimp a little on the Bailey's," smiled Greg as he looked down at the GPS. "Well I'll be a son of a bitch! It works! Not only that, but you pegged it," he exclaimed as he held out the GPS for J.P. to see.

Greg scanned the nearby shoreline while he took another sip from his mug. "I'm going to take the chainsaw and cut us up a couple of dry windfall trees just inside that tree line for kindling."

"OK den. I'll drill some holes and set a couple of lines den," said J.P. as he started unfastening the power ice auger from the front rack of Greg's vehicle.

Twenty minutes later Greg returned, skidding two long, dry cedars behind his ATV. He parked them in front of the hut. "This should keep our asses warm for now," he said stepping down from his bike.

As Greg took a few steps, J.P. couldn't help but notice him limping. "You had a little accident dere?"

Greg glanced at J.P. with a disgusted look. "Yeah, I slipped. I think I pulled a hamstring. It's just like a freaking skating rink under the snow up there."

J.P.'s eyes squinted as he tried to make sense of what Greg had said. "You mean on land?"

"Ya," replied Greg in a moody tone. "You would almost think that someone used a fire hose on the whole shoreline. It's glare fuckin' ice under that snow."

J.P. stared across at the shoreline in wonder. "Maybe dat ice could be from a broken beaver dam furder up dere?"

"Whatever. All I can say is, if you ever go there for a dump, hold onto a tree or you'll be wearing it. Hey, I thought you were going to set us up a couple of lines." Greg scanned the area, his brow furrowed.

J.P. looked to the left of Greg and then to his right. "Maudit!" he shouted as he ran over to one of the holes. He stood there, looking stunned. "I set dem lines only five minutes ago."

*It wasn't uncommon for a big fish to pull an untended fishing line through a hole in Lake Matinenda, but two at once?* Greg didn't doubt J.P. for a second as he walked up to their fishing hut and reached inside the door. He brought out a long gaff hook with a D-handle and hung it on a nail outside the hut. "OK, bring on the monsters," he chuckled.

# CHAPTER 10

Darren stood behind the bar at the Riverside Hotel. He sipped on a coffee, trying to look spry after a late night with Lori at the Lodge. He leafed through a newspaper. The Main Street door opened and sent a cold draft through his t-shirt. Darren looked up from the paper to see Big Bob. Darren was surprised to see him there so early. *Is he checking up on me?* he wondered.

"Good morning," boomed Bob, as he stomped his boots on the doormat, shaking off every flake of snow. He walked toward the bar, waving to a few regulars.

Bob squeezed his burly frame between Darren and the fridge while glancing down at Darren's paper. "So how old is the coffee?"

"Just made it," replied Darren still reading the paper.

"Any good news?" asked Bob as he poured himself a coffee.

Darren wasn't sure how to answer Bob. He probably knew that Darren had arrived back at the Riverside long after the bar had closed. *Or did Bob mean news in the paper?* "Na...I got back late from Matinenda last night."

"I kinda figured you were up there sniffing around."

"What do you mean by that?" replied Darren with a straight face.

"Oh, I heard from a few snowmobiles touring from Elliot Lake that they saw a new, silver Yamaha V.K. parked in front of the Lodge earlier last night." Darren was reminded that he was living in a small town and that he could run but he couldn't hide.

"Oh yah," he said with a smile. "I had a few games of pool with Lori after visiting with Greg and J.P. up on the north end."

Bob was surprised at the distance Darren had traveled. "You were at Greg's earlier?"

"Yeah. They said to say 'hi' to you and Derek."

"So how is Greg these days?"

"He was in a pissy mood when his radio wouldn't work last night." Darren scratched his head. "Come to think of it both of our GPSs weren't working either."

"GPSs?" replied Bob with a doubtful look.

"No shit, Bob. We know they run off of satellites. I even tried calling Greg's cell from the Lodge to let him know I made it back safely, but it was fucked up too."

Bob locked eyes with Darren. "That's really strange—the dispatcher for Blind River Taxi couldn't radio out to any of their cars because of the same bullshit. I ended up driving two couples home through that damn storm after I closed. Funny, one of them asked me if cell phones worked from here. Apparently all she could get were some freaky low tones on her phone when she tried calling for a cab. I thought she was just too drunk to make a call."

# CHAPTER 11

Kevin and John travelled west of Sudbury. John saw a highway billboard that read, "Welcome to 94.1 FM Moose music."

"Let's check it out, eh? I never heard *Moose* music before."

"It's probably a sister station of our station in North Bay. We should try and catch the local weather forecast."

John tuned the radio to 94.1 FM. Suddenly a low bass tone came over the speakers. John was startled by the sound and looked toward Kevin. "Well, my guess is that it's a bull moose in heat." They both laughed as Kevin scanned to another station. It was halfway into the Northern Ontario weather forecast. "*...and for the CBC listeners in the District of Elliot Lake, Blind River and Algoma, if you can receive* *us, we have been experiencing technical difficulties. It will remain clear for the rest of the night with an overnight low of minus twenty.*"

John looked over at Kevin. "Well I guess that explains the Moose music."

"Hey, is it me or am I imagining it?" asked Kevin looking into his side mirror.

"Imagining what?" muttered John as he reclined in his seat and closed his eyes.

"A lot of cop cars. I have one on my ass, one just drove by, and there was one parked at the Elliot Lake turnoff."

"Ah, just a coincidence." The words drifted up from John's direction, his body now curled up in a comfortable position, eyes closed.

Minutes later, Kevin glanced at John as they passed a "Welcome to Blind River" sign. "We're here. You can wake up now."

John started awake, opening his eyes and readjusting his seat. "I wasn't sleeping. I was just resting my eyes."

Kevin grinned. "Sure. Sure."

They approached an O.P.P. station with a helicopter parked on a pad and a larger than normal fleet of cruisers parked in the lot.

Kevin squinted. “What’s the population of Blind River?”

“Uh, around six or seven thousand?”

Kevin grinned, “Hmm…must be one hell of a tough town. Best we stay away from the nightlife. I heard that them big lumberjacks can sure whup your ass.”

The next half hour was spent picking up beer and snacks. As they approached a Tim Horton’s, they couldn’t help but notice a white cargo van with a satellite dish mounted on its roof and large CBC Radio decals on its side idling in the drive-thru.

“Must be their technicians from Sudbury tracking down their transmission problems.”

“You’re probably right Kevin. And they’ve always got time for Tim Horton’s. Turn right on the next street at the Royal Bank. That’s the main street.”

Kevin pulled his Jeep over to the Iron Horse Tavern. He slapped his stomach. “Good. I’m craving that liquid lunch and something to eat.”

• • •

Finishing their lunch and a liquor store visit, John and Kevin made their way back to the Jeep and set out for the rental shop.

"Now I'm ready to rock. Lunch sure as hell hit the spot. That was one hell of a good cheeseburger and fries."

John smirked. "You sure it wasn't that pitcher of beer you inhaled? My god, you looked happier than a pig in shit when that hot chick found you your Jack Daniels, or was it when she bent over?"

Kevin raised his liquor store bag. "Hell ... just you wait till I fix us up a thermos of hot toddies with this here stuff. You'll be happier than two pigs in shit."

They soon had two snowmobiles on a trailer hitched to the back of the Jeep. John stood in front of a glass counter with a shopping bag in his hand as a young female clerk processed his VISA card. Kevin was checking out an underwater ice fishing video camera. Electronic devices always intrigued him.

The clerk glanced up at John. "I'm really sorry about running out of minnows. We should have more in a day or two. But I'm sure that those jigs you bought should do the same trick."

Kevin pointed to the camera. "Excuse me, but how deep is that camera good for?"

"That Aqua-Vu is good for one hundred feet and has adjustable contrast and brightness, including infrared lights for low-light viewing…it'll also record and replay."

Kevin nodded. "That's one hell of a fishing aid."

"Yep, they're becoming very popular. The Lodge you're staying at purchased that same model from us. They are using it as one of their prizes for their fishing derby next month."

"One of their prizes?" replied John with a surprised look.

"Yep," she smiled, "I'm sure first prize is an ATV."

"Oh my god I wish we could make it," said Kevin.

"Is there any chance that you guys will be fishing at the north end of Matinenda?"

Her question caught the men off guard. There was a pause as Kevin glanced pointedly at John. "That was our plan for tomorrow morning."

"Well, a couple of guys are staying up in the north end and forgot their bait here yesterday. Would it be possible for you guys to drop it off to them?"

Kevin was quick to answer her. "Hell, we'd be more than happy to."

"Well, I'm sure that they'd be grateful. They're up for two weeks. We tried calling them on their cell but we get that same freaky sound we hear on the radio."

Kevin nodded in acknowledgement. "I know what you mean."

The young girl sighed. "It gets better. I just heard that emergency services radios aren't working half the time. Anyhow, I'll just grab the minnows from the back." She turned and disappeared behind a door marked "Staff."

"Are you fuckin' crazy?" John whispered. "We're supposed to keep under the radar."

"Are you kidding? This is a great way of getting on the inside," said Kevin as he grabbed two coils of snare wire from a box.

The girl returned carrying a small blue cooler. "This is their cooler. There are two plastic bags inside, one with suckers and one with minnows. They should be fine. I gave them oxygen…with ice. Keep them in your cabin tonight. It's supposed to get even colder overnight."

"So who are these guys we're looking for?" asked John.

"Their names are Greg and J.P. You won't miss them. Greg is a big Polish man and J.P. is a short Frenchman with a heavy accent. And they have a huge, white shanty at the end of the lake."

"Oh, I forgot," said Kevin holding up the snare wire.

The girl picked them out of Kevin's hand and dropped them into John's shopping bag with the rest of the fishing tackle. "Don't be crazy. You two spent enough here...and going out of your way like that...it's on the house."

Kevin pulled out of the rental driveway and headed north.

John moaned, his legs uncomfortably straddling the cooler.

Kevin smiled. "Ah, come on. It's not that bad, and besides, they might even loan us a few of them."

"I suppose so," said John as he cracked open the lid to take a peek. "Holy shit, those sucker minnows...what'd she call them—"suckers"?—are freakin' *huge*!"

"Ya...big bait for big fish. I'm starting to like these guys already," smiled Kevin.

John shut the cooler lid tight. "So what's with the snare wire?"

"Well, after she told us that the two of them occupied the north end, I thought that setting snares was a good reason for entering a tree line...in case they saw us and asked questions."

John was impressed by Kevin's quick thinking. "Good thinking," he said.

The landscape began to transform as the odd country home and hobby farm soon gave way to savage country where huge, snow-covered white pines dominated. John stared out his side window as the road took them past scenic frozen lakes and a meandering river that crossed under a collection of bridges. John could sense that Kevin was deep in thought. He hadn't spoken for some time. "Everything OK?"

There was a long silence.

"They're in a crisis situation."

John's eyes narrowed, confused as to what Kevin had said.

Kevin stared at the road as if in a trance.

"Who in the hell is '*they*'"?

There was a long pause. Kevin reached over and turned on the radio. That same low, spooky sound they heard earlier was back on. Kevin turned the radio off. "She said that freaky sound on the radio is the same one that was on the cell phone."

Bewildered, John pulled his cell out from his pocket and speed-dialed his apartment number. After hearing the low spooky tones he returned it to his pocket. There was another long silence. "That's bullshit. Cell phones are on a totally different frequency —they have their own towers."

"I *know*, but she also said that their ambulance radio had the same problem as well. That means that all emergency calls to the 9-1-1 dispatcher can't be radioed out through a dispatcher. So the police can only communicate by regular telephone or satellite phone."

"Holy shit. That would explain all those extra cop cars."

Kevin nodded with a grin. "That's right. It's like after Hurricane Katrina hit New Orleans—their biggest threat for emergency services was communication. The extra manpower in Blind River will keep the town less vulnerable to crime."

"Could you imagine this happening in a place like Toronto?"

"Chaos," asserted Kevin.

John smirked. "Are you kidding? It would be more like a fuckin' freak show. Chaos is when they get six inches of snow and call in the Army!"

## CHAPTER 12

A light breeze rattled the plexiglas window of the shack. Greg and J.P. sat looking out at the lake, their two fishing lines each tied to a thin, long branch that swayed in the wind. Two large lake trout lay on the ice outside the hut door. J.P. turned a sandwich over on the woodstove. "Well, I lost two lines but I caught two fish."

Greg knew he was trying to compensate for his earlier mishap. "So, I guess that makes you two for two then," he smirked as he poured a can of beans into a small pot.

"Don't worry Greg. I'll get you a new rod and reel when I get back to town, me."

"Don't be crazy. I'm just razzing you. I have three more at camp in the wood shed. Just remind me to bring them out tomorrow, as well as the rest of that lasagna. Darren said he would help us with it when he drops off the minnows."

"I can hardly wait to try out dem big suckers, me."

"Well," said Greg, "You did pretty good so far. You caught our limit on lake trout using jigs with pork rinds. Hey, maybe we'll snag a big pike."

J.P.'s sandwich started to smoke on the stove. He jumped up and lifted it off the stove.

"Yep, that's really something," said Greg as he put his pot of beans on the stove.

"What's dat?" asked J.P. taking a seat at the table.

"Oh...just you and me trying to keep warm up in Northern Ontario, eating burnt food in an eight by twelve shack...while our wives are sitting on the beach with them umbrella drinks and checking out all the young bucks."

"Well, I know for sure, me, dat my Marie will be hungry for me when she gets home dere," smiled J.P.

"You hope so," chuckled Greg. "We could be laying beside them checking out beavers while wearing dark, mirrored sun-glasses."

"No. I tink dat would be hard on me dere, trying to keep my tongue in my mout."

Greg laughed as he stirred his beans. "All kidding aside, I hope they can get through to us tonight or we'll just have to make a run to the Lodge and use their land phone. I have the number of the resort they're staying at."

J.P. looked at Greg. "You mean use old Charlie's phone?"

Greg was slow to answer. "Well...we have to let them know our cell phone is fucked up...and we don't want them to worry."

J.P. nodded. "Yes, I suppose you're right. At least it will get dem away from dem tall, dark men for a few minutes."

# CHAPTER 13

John sat slightly ahead in his seat like an excited child approaching a carnival.

"That last sign read 'Bear Head Lake' so Matinenda Lake should be just over this hill."

At the top of the crest, Kevin felt an unusual solitude as Lake Matinenda was exposed to them. Out in the distance, islands protruded through the white, snow-covered lake, the clear blue sky behind making for a breathtaking view. Kevin brought the Jeep to a stop and admired the view. Down to their right was a large parking lot serving a boat launch and docking area. The parking lot held a half a dozen or so vehicles.

To their left was a driveway that ran up on a slight incline to the Lodge, a large rustic two-storey building with a huge outdoor deck overlooking the lake.

"Oh my god," said John still on the edge of his seat.

"You mean more like 'God's country'," said Kevin as he began to follow the driveway to a parking area alongside the Lodge. After parking the Jeep, Kevin noticed rustic cabins scattered about. "Hmm...not too shabby."

As they left the Jeep, they noticed an elderly, white-bearded man wearing a red-checkered Elmer Fudd hunting jacket and hat, cleaning snow from the Lodge entrance.

"Excuse me sir!" shouted Kevin as they approached.

The elderly man stopped and looked their way.

"Are we OK to park here for a couple of minutes?"

The old-timer gave a gentle nod then blew his nose into a cloth hankie. "Are you two the ones from North Bay?" he asked in a friendly tone.

"Yes we are sir," replied Kevin.

"Welcome," he said as he held out his right hand to shake while still holding the hankie. Neither of the boys was quick to volunteer their hand to his used hankie. Finally he took notice of his hankie and returned it to his back pocket. "Pardon me. I'm Charley. Glad yous made it," he said giving each a firm handshake.

"Well I'm Kevin."

"And I'm John."

"I was going to call you Davy Crockett," he said as he looked up at Kevin's coonskin hat.

Kevin smiled. "Well at least you remembered the Alamo."

"Go ahead on in. Lori will give you your cabin key." He pointed up to the Lodge entrance.

Upon entering the Lodge the sound of wood crackling in a fireplace caught their attention. Trophy heads of deer, moose and bear, as well as large fish covered most of the knotty pine walls. A pool table sat in the middle of the large room with tables scattered throughout. A long bar made from pine logs stood along the far wall.

John pointed across the room to a walk-around counter with an open doorway behind it. "That must be the reception desk."

Faint strains of a rock and roll song could be heard as they approached the counter. Kevin noticed an Aqua-Vu on a shelf above the counter. A poster hung above it, promoting the Lodge's annual fishing derby. The same wall had countless photographs of guests proudly holding up their prize catch of fish or kneeling beside a trophy buck.

John helped himself to a Lodge brochure from a holder on top of the counter. He tapped his fingers on the counter to the beat of the rock song as he leafed through the brochure while Kevin gazed at the photos.

Suddenly, the men heard a female voice accompanying the song. It seemed to be coming from below the counter. John leaned slightly over the counter to take a look. He was taken by what he saw. He looked toward Kevin with a smile and pointed over the counter.

Out of curiosity Kevin stepped over to the counter and peered down. He first noticed long, blonde hair belonging to a girl who was cleaning out a shelf. She had a black cord that led from a set of earphones down her short T-shirt to an iPod that clipped to the side of her low-cut jeans.

The boys couldn't help but notice the black string of a thong running up through the crack of her rounded buttocks and out above the girl's jeans. The young men's eyes locked on her as she slowly swayed her shapely hips from side to side to the rhythm of the song.

Kevin pointed out a small sign that was taped just below a bell on the counter that read, "Pléase ring bell for service." John shook his head to Kevin's gesture, ogling the sexy view a little longer. Kevin reached out a flat hand over the bell as John desperately shook his head vigorously. Kevin hit the bell hard enough to make sure it would be heard over her loud music.

The singing abruptly stopped as she stood up from behind the counter. The boys couldn't help but notice her breasts under her low-cut, tight T-shirt. She blushed as she removed her earphones. "Oh! Sorry guys. I hope you weren't waiting long. I'm used to singing with a radio in the background but our local station has been acting strange lately."

"So we've heard," said Kevin, reaching his hand out to shake hers as he locked eyes with this tall, beautiful, blue-eyed blonde. "Hi. My name is Kevin. By the way, you have a beautiful voice."

Lori's face flushed slightly with this tall, handsome, robust man's introduction as he gently shook her hand. His eyes were keen and sharp. There was a steely confidence about Kevin that Lori liked and she returned his eye contact. "Well I'm Lori and I'm pleased to meet you," she said, smiling.

John waited patiently on the sidelines. He cleared his throat trying to get their attention. "You two on a first-name basis already?"

"Oh, I'm sorry Lori. This is my friend John."

"Pleased to meet you," she said as they shook hands. "How was the trip from North Bay?" she asked as she brought out a key from a drawer and handed it to Kevin.

"The roads were clear all the way."

"Your cabin is the second one on the left," she said with a warm smile.

"Thanks. Oh...what time is dinner?" smiled Kevin.

"Whatever time you guys want. I have a small snowmobile tour coming in late from

Elliot Lake. They will have eaten already so you two are my only customers for dinner."

Kevin looked at John. "How does six sound?"

"Fine by me."

Kevin gazed into her deep blue eyes. "Can we eat at the bar?"

Lori flushed. "You two can eat anywhere you like."

"All right. At the bar at six," said Kevin as he and John headed towards the exit.

Kevin glanced over at John as they made their way back to the Jeep. "I'm sure as hell anxious to get them there sleds out for a test ride."

John grinned. "Are you kidding me? I thought you would be interested in test-riding something else. She's freakin' hot…and I think she likes you…her rack is 'volumptuous'," said John holding out his hands from his chest for effect.

Kevin smirked at John's mispronunciation. "No John…I think you mean, 'voluptuous'?"

John shook his head. "No Kevin, they are 'VOLUMMMMPTUOUS!", this time holding out his hands much further from his chest to make his point.

Kevin blushed at John's sign language and pushed John into a snow bank. "Now that should cool your jets for a while!"

Kevin laughed as he watched John struggle to get his footing in the deep snow.

## CHAPTER 14

Kevin leaned over the pool table and took a few practice strokes with his cue. "I'm gonna go cross side with the black."

Lori watched from behind the bar as she set down two beer next to a basket of Buffalo chicken wings.

John watched intently from a bar stool as he nibbled on a wing.

Kevin took the shot.

John's eyes followed the cue ball as it hit the black ball off the bank and rolled across the table straight into the side pocket. John swiveled his seat to face Lori and dropped a chicken bone on his plate. "That's bullshit!"

"No," replied Kevin, hanging up his cue with a smirk. "It's more like three out of four."

Lori pointed down to a map on the bar. "Like I said, the only bad spot is through

Graveyard Narrows. Just stick to your left and giv'er."

"Yeah, and then try and find Greg and J.P.," muttered Kevin as he sat down next to John.

Lori arched her penciled brows. "So how do you two know Greg and J.P.?"

Kevin grabbed a wing from the basket. "Oh, it's a long story."

"Well, this bar doesn't close until two A.M."

"They forgot their minnows back at the U-Rental Bait and Tackle shop where we rented our sleds."

"Oh my god," said Lori as she laughed.

Kevin looked at John. "Did we miss something?"

Lori shook her head with a big smile. "I know someone that was going to drop them off at their cottage later tomorrow."

"Well at least them boys will be able to use their bait first thing tomorrow morning," said Kevin as he took a swig of beer.

"They're sold out of minnows and might be getting some more in. Do you think your friend would mind picking up a couple of dozen for us?" asked John.

"Sure," said Lori as she picked up a phone. "I'll call Darren to let him know."

Kevin looked over at John as he dropped a bone on his plate. "I told you, everyone knows everyone in these small towns."

John nodded in agreement. "So...are you excited for your first real run on a snowmobile tomorrow?"

Kevin exhaled slightly as he looked down at the map. "I'd have to say that it's Graveyard Narrows that scares the crap out of me."

John chuckled as he patted Kevin on his shoulder. "Don't worry. You did good this afternoon when we brought the sleds out on that test run."

Lori hung up the phone. "So I got a hold of Darren and told him about the minnow situation. He hopes to meet up with you two on the north end later tomorrow morning and said he'd check for minnows for you as well."

"Well that's nice of him to go out of his way for us," said Kevin.

Lori locked eyes with Kevin. "Up here we believe what goes around, comes around."

Hours later the rumbling sound of small engines could be heard approaching the Lodge as headlight beams flashed through the front windows. Lori glanced down at her watch. "That must be the snowmobile tour from Elliot Lake. I'm going to leave you two for a few minutes so I can give them their cabin keys." She turned on the TV behind the bar. A fuzzy picture appeared with the same spooky low tone that Kevin and John had heard on the car radio earlier that day.

"Holy shit," Kevin said under his breath. "It's affecting TV signals as well."

Lori turned the set off and laid the remote down on the bar and looked at Kevin. "Yep, it's sporadic, just like the radio and cell phones. Darren told me that a CTV news crew was in Blind River to cover the story today. I was hoping to catch it later on the eleven o'clock news. Oh well, if I miss it he'll fill me in," she said as she started to leave.

Kevin swiveled his bar stool to follow her. "Excuse me Lori . . ."

Lori stopped and looked back at Kevin. He had a confused look about him. "Yes?"

"You said that Darren would fill you in on the eleven o'clock news?"

"Oh, I'm sorry. He's got cable. We're on antenna."

Kevin nodded with a dumb smile. "Thank you," he said as he swiveled his stool back in position.

Ten minutes later Lori was back behind the bar, opening two beers for Kevin and John who were back at the pool table.

Three elderly men walked into the Lodge and made their way towards the bar. The lead man was short and stocky. He walked as far as the pool table and stopped. He looked over at Kevin and John. "Excuse me boys but are you the two hillbillies that own that Jeep that's parked in front of that first cabin?"

The boys could tell from his looks that he had started hitting the bottle already.

"Well, I'm from Kentucky," said Kevin.

The elderly man held out his hand to shake. "I'm Tom McClenny. Me and my friends are Wolverines from Houghton Lake, Michigan. The other three young bucks crawled in for the night. So, you sure as hell came a long way to sled," he said as he and his buddies made their way to the bar. "So Lori, where in the hell is the old buckeye?" Tom muttered.

"Oh, Charley crashed shortly after nine but he'll be up at six with a fresh pot of coffee waiting for you, Tom." She sat their beers down.

John and Kevin could hear Tom's loud, impaired voice as he dominated the conversation at the bar.

Tom's eyes narrowed as he looked across at Lori. "What the hell do you think is causing all this radio wave or electronic interference around in these parts? We couldn't use our communicators on this side of Vance's Motor Inn in Spanish." Tom paused. He patted the back of the fellow to his right. "Steve here tried to call this Lodge on his cell phone from the parking lot at the Fireside Inn in Elliot Lake and got that same freaky deep sound we got on our communicators."

Steve nodded in agreement while taking a swig of beer.

Lori locked eyes with Tom. You're right. Apparently most of Algoma is affected almost to the Soo."

Tom whined. "Well that's just great. I won't be able to communicate to my buddies all the way to the Water Tower Inn in Sault Ste. Marie."

Steve smiled. "I don't think any of us are complaining."

There was a pause. Old Tom's face tightened, as he looked at Steve. "Now don't be a smart ass," he said, as everyone laughed.

"A television news crew was in Blind River today to cover these strange stories," said Lori as she pressed the TV remote power button. A clear picture appeared. "See what I mean? It's working good now."

Steve took out his cell phone and turned it on. "Yep. I have service," he said as he looked over at Tom.

Tom was preoccupied, scanning the map of Lake Matinenda that Kevin and John had left on the bar. Tom pointed down to a spot on the map. "This is the spot where we really needed the use of our communicators, that was where Arnold first stopped his sled."

"Did he have a mechanical problem?" asked Lori.

Steve rolled his eyes. "Huh! More like a mental problem."

"Arnold kept insisting that he was being followed by a glowing light from under the ice," chuckled Tom.

"Yeah, he did this three freakin' times until we made him run second from the lead," said Steve.

Tom smiled at Lori. "You should ask him at breakfast if he was the one that saw the light."

Steve shook his head. "No, I think the last light Arnold saw was in the parking lot at the Fireside Inn, back in Elliot Lake, when he drank that flask of Jack Daniels."

Minutes later Lori turned up the volume on the television as the late news was about to air. All eyes were glued to the tube.

A CTV reporter was standing in a parking lot of the Blind River OPP station next to a police officer.

"*I'm here in Blind River with Sergeant Henry Buchanan who is with the Ontario Provincial Police. There have been a lot of reports of electronic malfunctions affecting reception for radio, television, cell phones and wireless computer routers. Could you comment on this?*"

*"Yes Gord. It first started with the odd complaint but has now grown to be a major problem. As far as emergency services are concerned, we have reason to believe that all radio signal interruptions have been caused by cell phone hackers. It's a cyber security warning for everyone to watch out for crooks that are redirecting connections to fake websites. It's technically called 'drive-by pharming.' By using a wireless router device, they drive by and redirect connections to fake websites that resemble places such as Ebay, banks, and Paypal. So once the consumer enters their confidential data in the fake site, the criminals can then start draining their accounts."*

*"So is there a way of safe guarding ourselves against 'drive-by pharming?'"*

*"Yes Gord...by entering new passwords for the defaulted passwords that are supplied with routers. We believe it's the work of about ten or more sophisticated hackers that are presently working in the Algoma district as a test market, so to speak. It's a combination of all their signals that have caused this wide*

*band, which is causing the interruptions. Police are asking the public to report anyone in the area that may look suspicious to Crimestoppers at 1-800-222-TIPS."*

*"Thank you Sergeant Buchanan ...we will continue to follow the story as it unfolds. Gord Nicholls, CTV News, Blind River."*

Tom swiveled around on his bar stool and looked across at Kevin and John who were watching the news. "Well, it does seem a little suspicious when a hillbilly travels this far from Kentucky just to snowmobile!"

Lori nodded. "That's right. They did ask me if we had Internet service for a laptop."

Everyone laughed.

A big smile grew on Kevin's face. "I would have to agree with you on that one Tom!"

# CHAPTER 15

The next morning, John and Kevin were back in the Lodge, sharing a breakfast table with Charley as Lori topped up their coffees.

"You mean to say we missed them?" asked Kevin adding a creamer to his coffee.

"I don't think you missed Tom's loud mouth," smiled Charley, as he raised his cup to his lips.

Lori was busy picking up dirty dishes. "Yeah, last night he did seem to get louder by the drink."

Kevin reached over the table and handed his dirty plate to add to Lori's pile. "So, did you ask their buddy who kept stopping his snowmobile, and holding them up, if he was the one that saw the light?"

Lori raised her brows. "As a matter of fact, I did. And as much as they claimed he had a lot to drink, he still swears on seeing a light under the ice."

"Hmm...it was probably a reflection of a headlight from behind him," said John.

"No, because he was the sweeper," replied Lori.

"The 'sweeper'?" asked Kevin with a confused look.

"Yes. That's what they call the last sled that follows at the back. On tours, he's like a safety in case anyone breaks down. But when you're night riding you never advance, unless you can see the light of the snowmobile behind you in your mirror. And the fact that they couldn't use their communicators only pissed off his buddies when they had to continually turn back for him." Lori walked away from the table with a tray of dirty dishes.

Kevin nodded. "Oh ya, Tom mentioned that."

Charley took a sip from his cup. "So when you two meet up with Greg and J.P., tell them I said 'Hi' and to drop by for a couple of cold ones on me."

"I'll do that Charley," said Kevin as he and John got up from their chairs. "Oh, and can you thank Lori for the awesome breakfast?"

Charley pointed up from his chair. "You could thank her yourself."

Lori was standing next to him holding out a paper bag.

"What's this?" asked Kevin with a surprised look.

"Oh, it's just a little something for you two to snack on later today."

Kevin shook his head with a warm smile. "This is too much."

"Go ahead and take it. She doesn't do that for just anyone. Trust me," said Charley.

A blush appeared on Lori's face as she handed Kevin the bag. "So what time and what would you two like for dinner?" she asked holding out two menus.

Kevin held his hand out like a traffic cop. "Hell no…nothing fancy. If we can have some more of that there pub grub, at around six o'clock that would be just fine by me."

"Well, good luck fishing boys. I hope you'll have a good fish story to tell me tonight," said Charley as he got up from the table.

It was bitter cold outside as John rummaged through a pile of gear in the back of the Jeep.

A dark green army pack with two fishing rods protruding out from it caught Kevin's attention. "It's over there," he pointed.

John handed the pack to Kevin with a big smile. "I think she's got the hots for you!"

"You reckon?" replied Kevin, grabbing the pack from John.

"Ohhhh, yaaa...Who could miss that big blush of hers when she handed you that lunch bag," said John as he punched Kevin's shoulder. John struggled with his ice chisel as it found its way to the bottom of the gear. He noticed that a large green metal army ammo box was pinning it down. "What in the hell did you pack in that box?"

There was a pause.

Kevin looked uneasy. "Oh, that's the surprise that I mentioned to you back in North Bay."

John's stomach sank as he flipped open a heavy metal snap on each end and removed the lid. A shocked look grew on his face as he peered into the box. "Are you fucking *crazy*? Do you realize what would happen to us if we were caught with this in our possession?"

Kevin frowned and spoke as calmly as possible. "Now don't go ballistic on me. I can explain how it got there."

John groaned. "This better be good."

Kevin chuckled nervously. "I mentioned to Bill in the Armories that I needed just a little bit of plastic explosives to remove a few boulders that block a roadway up at a friend's cottage and he loaded this into the back of the Jeep when we were working our last shift. He told me to take what I needed and he would take back the rest."

"So then what happened?"

"He was called over to the Petawawa base to work for a week."

John was still confused as to Kevin's motive. "Now back up for a second. What was the reason for wanting explosives in the first place?"

"Well you know I had that advanced training with explosives in the U.S Army?"

"Yes," said John, as he followed along.

"I just thought that since we had to venture out so far to hunt down that meteor, that it would sure be nice if we could take us back a wee sample of that thing, or we might even need a little bit of explosives to coax it out from a crevice or something like that."

There was a pause. John sighed deeply. "OK Kevin, but if we get caught, all this shit is yours."

# CHAPTER 16

John and Kevin cruised across Lake Matinenda in the frigid cold, with John in the lead. John brought his snowmobile to a sudden stop and killed the engine. Kevin pulled up alongside him and did the same. John pointed over his windshield. "That's *gotta* be Graveyard Narrows straight ahead."

John pulled out his GPS. After viewing it for a few seconds he slapped it against his leg.

"What's wrong?" Kevin asked.

"Hell if I know. It just went all squirrelly on me."

"Huh...that's odd. You just had it working earlier at the cabin. It must be the batteries."

John shook his head. "Not! I just put new ones in and the power level indicator says 'good'." He frowned as he returned it to his pocket. "Now how in the hell are we supposed to hunt for that meteor?"

Kevin slapped his large parka pocket and grinned. "There's a new invention out called a map and compass and 'X' marks the spot!"

"You bastard," laughed John as he started his machine. "Now remember what Lori said; when we get to the Narrows, stick to the left and 'giv'er'!"

Minutes later, after passing through the dangerous channel, John stopped his sled and killed the engine as Kevin pulled up beside him. John lifted his visor and raised his chin, sniffing the cold air like a bloodhound.

"Is everything OK?" asked Kevin.

"Do you smell anything?"

Kevin raised his visor and took a big whiff. "No...not really."

"Well I thought maybe you shit your pants when we drove past that large, open hole in the Narrows!" chuckled John.

A grin appeared on Kevin's face. "No, but I sure as hell came awfully close!"

Looking across at the north shore John spotted two structures on the ice. "It looks like a couple of fishing huts on the north end. Let's check it out."

Greg was outside the hut jigging over a hole when he noticed two snowmobiles approaching. "I think we're getting some visitors," he hollered to J.P.

John and Kevin brought their sleds down to a crawl and pulled up alongside the shanty. They noticed a big man wearing a beaver skin hat who fit Greg's description to a 'T'. John gave them a casual wave as they killed their engines. The large backpack that was strapped to Kevin's sled and their white army apparel was enough to convince Greg that they weren't police or conservation officers.

Kevin pointed down to a large lake trout lying on the ice. "Nice fish!"

"Thanks. I just caught it," said Greg.

As J.P. stepped out from the shanty, his brow furrowed. He had noticed a blue cooler just like Greg's fastened to the back of Kevin's sled.

"Good morning," said John as he stood from his sled. "I think we have something that belongs to you."

Greg and J.P. watched Kevin unfasten a bungee cord that secured the cooler.

"Is dat a present from Darren?" asked J.P.

Kevin handed the cooler to J.P. "No sir, but Lori from the Lodge said that he'll be joining you two for lunch later this afternoon. Me and my partner picked it up yesterday at the U-Rental place in Blind River."

"Well thank you very much!" said Greg as he held his hand out to greet them. "Now come on into the shack and warm yourselves up. We've got some coffee on the go."

The men stomped inside the cozy fishing shack, bonding together for a good hour over coffee spiked with brandy.

"Yes Greg," said Kevin. "It was Lori who told us that Darren had planned on dropping them there minnows off to you'all this afternoon."

Greg smiled back at Kevin. "So...you two met Lori. She's a sweetie isn't she?"

Kevin nodded. "Yes sir...I think she's a real good asset for Old Charley."

"I think you mean a nice looking ass to have around," chuckled Greg. "You should see her in the summer when she's pumping gas down at the dock in these little shorts. They're so tight you can read her lips. The local boys don't care how much Charley sells his gas for just as long as she's pumping it. Old Bill from Ohio walked off the dock and into the lake when she bent over. He told his wife that he tripped on a board!"

Everyone burst out laughing.

Greg pointed up at a large, foil roasting pan on the shelf. "So how about helping us with that lasagna my wife made?"

John glanced at the large roasting pan. "Holy shit...she made enough to feed a freakin' army!"

Greg leaned forward and pointed to the Canadian Forces crest on John's parka. "Well...it looks like you two are dressed for the occasion so why don't you join us for lunch when Darren drops by?" He grabbed his bottle of brandy and proceeded to top up their coffees.

Kevin shook his head and placed a hand over his coffee mug. "No thanks...I've had enough."

"Oh come on Kevin. Just let me 'Canadianize' it a little!"

Kevin and John laughed. "Hell Greg," said Kevin. "If I have one more of them there 'Canadianized' coffees I'll be crawling back to the Lodge."

Suddenly J.P. jumped up from his chair and rushed out the door.

Looking through the window onto the lake, John noticed a long branch, bent in half, down a fishing-hole. "Holy shit," he shouted in amazement. He sprang up from his chair and bolted out the door.

Greg calmly stood up and walked out of the shack. He grabbed the gaff that hung on the outside wall. "Give 'em lots of line!" he hollered.

J.P. was only at arm's length when he saw his line snap. "Maudit!" he yelled. His rage was visible to Kevin and John.

"Don't tell me you lost your friend again? If it wasn't for that radio playing you would have heard your drag screaming," chuckled Greg while tapping the gaff against his leg.

J.P. was down on one knee unfastening his fishing rod and reel from a large branch that was anchored into the ice.

John was impressed with J.P.'s heavy-duty rig. He spoke quietly. "You mean to tell me that fish peeled off all your line and snapped it?"

"Yep…all one hundred feet of fifty pound test," Greg muttered.

J.P. looked uneasy. He held his right hand sideways as though he was about to make a karate chop and pointed due west. "Dat fish went dat way."

John shrugged with a doubtful look. "How do you know that?"

"From de way de line bent before it broke."

John nodded in acknowledgement.

Greg could see John's enthusiasm. "So, now will you two be joining us?"

"Sure, but if you don't mind, we want to set a few rabbit snares inside that tree line." He pointed.

"No problem…but take your snowmobiles. I'm pretty sure you're required to have a small game license to set rabbit snares. If a conservation officer shows up, just tell him that you're hunting for firewood."

"Thanks for the alibi," replied Kevin.

Greg pointed. "You'll see my tracks from yesterday. I have a trail entering in just to the right of that cedar tree and come to think of it, I did see a couple of good rabbit trails back there."

"You better watch the hice," said J.P.

Kevin's eyes narrowed. "Hice?" he repeated.

Greg chuckled. "J.P. meant to say 'ice'. Some French Canadians can't pronounce the letter 'I' in English. That's why the Montreal Canadiens have a big 'CH' in the middle of their hockey rink. It stands for Centre 'hice'!" The men groaned. "All kidding aside, he's right. For some unknown reason it's glare ice under the snow over there. I slipped yesterday."

"Thanks for the warning," said John as they climbed onto their snowmobiles.

"Me and J.P. will be drilling some extra fishing holes for later. Is there any place in particular you two would like yours?"

Kevin held his hand out sideways like J.P. did earlier and pointed due west.

"Right on!" smiled Greg giving Kevin the thumbs-up.

## CHAPTER 17

The sound of Greg's power ice auger caught Kevin and John's attention as they removed their helmets

"They're quite the guys," smiled John as he looked toward the shack from the shoreline.

"Hell, I'll say! And J.P is something else with that French Canadian accent."

John nodded. "Yeah, and they really know their shit in the outdoors."

Suddenly the ice cracked like thunder and shifted beneath their feet. Without hesitation, Kevin took two long strides and dived onto the shoreline. His body landed hard, knocking the wind from him as he slid back down to where John was standing. Not making any effort to stand, he took a deep breath then slowly looked up at John and moaned. "What in the fuck happened?"

John exploded in laughter and reached out a hand. "The extra holes that Greg drilled released pressure from the ice."

Kevin grabbed John's outstretched hand and slowly stood. "Well it sure as hell scared the shit out of me. J.P. was right about the 'hice'," he said as he looked back at his skid marks on the glare ice behind him. "I wonder what caused it?" he said as he pulled out his GPS. "Well I'll be a son of a bitch. It's working again!" Kevin held out the GPS to John. "Check it out. We must have horseshoes up our asses!" He pointed up at the slope behind them. "It's up on that ridge about a hundred yards."

"I can hardly wait to see it," said John as he pulled out the ice chisel from his sled.

Kevin looked skeptical. "Tell me that isn't for snow snakes."

John just smirked as he watched Kevin cautiously step up off the lake onto Greg's trail, grabbing large limbs and small trees to steady his balance. John followed close behind, using his long ice chisel as a walking stick.

Not five minutes into their hike up, Kevin held up his hand and stopped dead in his tracks. He tilted his head sideways to assist his hearing while he pointed to a snow-covered cedar thicket ten feet in front of them. Kevin held his index finger to his lips, indicating to John not to speak, as he eased his way towards the thicket.

John had no idea what had alarmed Kevin but he followed cautiously with his two hands firmly holding up his long ice pick like an Olympic pole-vaulter, ready for whatever might lurk inside the thicket.

Suddenly, a loud and deep pulsating sound came from the cedars, as snow flew up from the thick boughs. Kevin jolted backwards and landed on his buttocks as he caught a glimpse of a large, brown bird flushing towards the ridge.

Kevin turned to look back at John and found himself staring down at the razor sharp point of John's ice chisel just inches from his face.

"Those freakin' partridge can scare the hell out of ya!" scoffed John as he scanned the ridge.

The excitement of finding the meteor drove them on as they trudged through the deep snow. It was hard, sweaty work, the men having to lift their legs high to make any headway through the tall drifts.

"Fuckin' shit", John exclaimed. After what seemed like hours of hiking, John, who had been leading the trek, finally came to a stop. He gave a nervous chuckle as Kevin caught up to him. He was pointing down with his ice chisel at some tracks: Their old tracks. The fact that they had walked in a big circle didn't rest well with either man.

"That's freakin' bullshit!" Kevin scoffed as he glanced down at his GPS. There was a long silence. "I don't know what to tell you John, other that my GPS is working fine. Look, I'll show you." Kevin knelt down on one knee and opened his map on the snow and then placed his compass in line with the due north. "Now see for yourself. The compass isn't lying. It's the same reading as my GPS."

"Is there any way there is some kind of mistake from your computer print-out?" asked John.

Kevin glanced up with a stunned look. "No!"

"Well maybe that meteorite hit here and deflected off and landed somewhere else."

John's theory took Kevin by surprise. Kevin nodded. "You just may have something there. But I'd like to go over the crash site again on my laptop tonight. I'm sure it wasn't much of a trajectory."

Kevin's fatigue was visible to John. He reached down and patted Kevin's shoulder. "So in the meantime what do you say we set a few snares and help J.P. catch that monster?"

# CHAPTER 18

When Kevin and John parked their sleds in front of Greg's fishing shack they were surprised to see a new, silver snowmobile already parked there.

Greg and J.P. stepped out from the shanty to greet them, each holding a paper plate with a large piece of lasagna. Greg was chewing a mouthful as he looked down onto the ice and gently nudged a clear plastic bag of minnows with his boot.

"So Darren made it," said Kevin replacing his helmet with his coonskin hat.

"That's funny," said John. "We never heard him arrive."

Greg pointed his fork at Darren's sled as he swallowed. "That's because it's a four stroke."

"It looks like a Fur Hat Fashion Show!" said a voice from the doorway.

Kevin and John looked up at a young man about their age with a beer in hand, who also wore a fur hat.

Greg cocked his head as he stroked the side of his hat. "Yes Darren...most of us Northern boys prefer our heads inside a warm beaver, but I'm surprised that J.P. hasn't eaten his."

They all laughed.

J.P. stepped forward and looked up at Kevin's coonskin hat. "I never looked at a hat in the eyes before, me." Then J.P. glanced up at John's hat. "But I remember when dey gave twenty-five dollar for de ears of John's timber wolf hat, dere."

Greg nodded. "Yes J.P. but that bounty was scrapped shortly after."

"Was it because they killed too many timber wolves?" John asked.

"No," said Greg with a straight face. They had too many fuckin' earless German shepherds walking around in Northern Ontario that year."

Darren and John hunched over with laughter.

After introducing themselves and setting their fishing lines Kevin and John enjoyed their hot lunch out on the ice. "I feel bad that we didn't touch any of the lunch that Lori packed for us," said Kevin.

"She packed a lunch for you two?" asked Darren with a surprised look.

"Yes. That was real nice of her especially when it was not a part of our lodging package," said Kevin.

John nudged Kevin with his elbow. "Well, old Charley did say that she doesn't do that for everyone."

Kevin glanced at Darren and quickly changed the subject. "We'll just have to pick at that lunch later after we work up an appetite hauling out J.P.'s monster."

"For sure...I'm ready for him, dis time," said J.P.

"That's for sure," replied Greg. "He even drilled a hole and set a line in the shack so he wouldn't have to run."

Kevin nodded. "I saw it...and I also noticed he turned off the radio so he can hear his reel squeal when his friend strips the line from it."

Greg shook his head. "No. It was another

one of those interruptions again. We were hoping to get a news update on that Air Canada jet that was forced to make an emergency landing at the Sudbury Airport last night."

Kevin and John stared up at Greg. John spoke first, "Did they mention what kind of trouble the plane had?"

"Apparently part of its wing fell off," said Greg.

Kevin pulled his cell phone from his parka pocket. "I'll get to the bottom of this," he said as he turned it on.

Greg looked over at John. "What's he doing?"

"Oh...he's calling our buddies at NORAD for an update. NORAD always helps in emergency situations like this."

Greg's eyes narrowed. "Hmm . . ."

Kevin pulled his cell down from his ear. "Son of a bitch. It's that damn interference again."

Greg grinned. "That's why we have the radio turned off."

Kevin rolled his eyes and nodded. "You're right," he said as he returned the cell phone to his pocket.

"Yep...it's just like our GPSs," said Darren. "They won't work either when we have that interruption."

Kevin grinned. "Sorry Darren, but a GPS works off a satellite signal, which is totally independent from other radio signals." He pulled out his GPS, turned it on and held it face-up for everyone to see. To Kevin's surprise his viewing screen was all scrambled like John's had been earlier that morning.

Both Darren and Greg mutely held out their GPSs to Kevin. "It's been the same story since last night," Darren explained.

J.P. stepped into the shack and turned on the radio to low volume to let Kevin hear the low, spooky tone. "Now when dat noise goes away on da radio check dat GPS or your phone. You will see den it works."

There was a pause. Kevin stared toward the fishing hut and listened to the strange tones on the radio. "That's freaky." He put his GPS into his pocket in silence.

"You think *that's* bullshit," said Darren unscrewing the cap off a beer bottle. "You should come to town and listen to some of my customers in the Riverside. There's been crazy stories of remote car starters, garage door openers and alarms going off by themselves at all hours of the night. It's driving the owner of Home Hardware crazy. He's crying in his beer every night because customers are demanding a refund on their remote garage door openers. Some seniors even swear that Blind River is haunted."

Kevin smirked. "Huh...well there's more than one way to skin a cat. I'll e-mail my buddy Roger at NORAD first thing when we get back to the Lodge. I should be able to show you boys on my laptop tomorrow what exactly happened to that Air Canada passenger plane." Kevin pointed across to the other fishing shack. "Are they friends of yours?"

Greg shrugged. "Damned if I know. Your guess is as good as mine. It was there when we arrived yesterday."

"It'll probably be occupied this weekend," said Darren as he raised his beer to his lips.

"Holy shit!" Kevin hollered as he nudged John off to one side and ran towards his fishing hole.

The boys could see his rod bending in half. His reel screamed as line peeled off.

Kevin threw his mitts onto the ice and grabbed his rod out from its holder. "It's a monster!" he hollered while cranking his reel.

"I'll get the gaff," said Greg as the boys rushed to Kevin's side. Every few seconds line peeled off that Kevin had worked to retain.

"Tighten your drag a little more," said Darren.

Kevin glanced up. "I'm sorry but I only have twelve-pound test."

"You're doing fine. Just keep reeling," said Greg in a reassuring way as he stood calmly at Kevin's side, gaff in hand.

All eyes were glued to the hole when suddenly a dark shadow appeared at the bottom.

"Now keep it steady and move over just a bit," said Greg as he slowly lowered the gaff into the dark hole.

"*Maudit!!*" yelled J.P. as he bolted towards the fishing hut. His short legs moved like pistons, carrying his small frame toward the hut as the sound of his fishing reel drag echoed inside.

"Well holy shit! A double-hitter!" hollered Darren.

"OK, I got it," said Greg, down on his knees, as he skillfully pulled out a huge lake trout from Kevin's hole and laid it on the ice. Greg high-fived Kevin. "Good show!" Kevin slowly exhaled while a huge smile grew on his face.

"OK Kevin, hold that trout up! This one's for your ma!" said John aiming his digital camera at the proud fisherman and his catch.

The Kodak moment was broken by some powerful French cursing coming from the hut, words unlike any Greg had heard before. His eyes narrowed. "What the hell?" Greg quickly made his way towards the shack, gaff still in hand. He entered the hut and saw J.P. down on his knees peering into the dark hole.

J.P. turned his head slowly as he held up his jigging rod –all the line had stripped off the spool. "Dat's not a fish," he said with a frightened look.

"Oh come on J.P. You'll just have to go back to fishing school," laughed Darren as he peered around the doorway.

J.P. slowly got up from his knees. "I never saw dat before, me, but whatever it is, you can't stop it."

Greg smiled as he patted J.P.'s shoulder. "I can see that your friend is going to be quite the challenge for us. Let's have a cold one and let the young blood put the meat on the table."

"Hell Greg, I'm awfully sorry but I don't think I have any more horseshoes up my ass. I'll just pass the ball to Darren and John," said Kevin.

Darren handed Kevin a beer. "Well then...lets just celebrate that monster you have laying out on the ice."

As Kevin went to unscrew the cap, the bottle slipped out from his wet hands and fell onto the floor, rolling towards J.P.'s fishing hole. Kevin tried to grab it but Greg's big frame got in his way. They watched helplessly as it fell down the hole. "God damn!" Kevin scoffed.

Darren chuckled as he handed Kevin another beer and glanced down at the hole. "Let's call that one a sacrifice to J.P.'s monster for being such a sport. This one's for yours!"

# CHAPTER 19

Early in the evening in the main Lodge, the earthly aroma of maple burning in the fireplace lingered in the air as an old rock and roll song played in the jukebox. Twenty or so snowmobilers sat in the Lodge, the hum of conversation and the clink of glasses adding to the warm atmosphere.

"Black in the corner," said Kevin, hunched over the pool table.

John took a swig from his beer as he watched the cue ball strike the black, sending it slowly into the corner pocket. He rolled his eyes and high-fived Kevin. "Well, that's great. I thought you left the rest of your bullshit back at Greg's ice shack!"

Lori set down a couple of beers. "This is for your first lake trout through the ice," she said with a warm smile as she returned to the bar.

John whispered. “Oh boy, she still has that sexy smile for you.”

Kevin smirked. “Shut up and rack ‘em up.”

“Heard you did quite well for your first time at hard-water angling,” said a familiar voice from behind.

Kevin turned around to face old Charley, holding out his hand to congratulate him.

“Call it beginner’s luck,” said John, racking up the balls.

“How’d you like it, Kevin?” asked Charley.

“Well…I would say that ice-fishing is as close as you can get to not fishing while actually doing it!”

“Now that sure as hell would describe it,” chuckled Charley.

“And as for them there Graveyard Narrows, I would have to say it was a white knuckle experience.”

“I’ll catch up with you two later. Hope your luck carries on tomorrow,” said Charley as he made his way to the bar.

"Look what the cat dragged in," said John looking towards the main entrance as Darren, Greg, and J.P. made their way toward the pool table. "It's nice to see you guys made it out."

"We thought it would be a lot easier using my calling card on a land line than to take a chance of getting cut off the cell phone. Gotta keep track of our ladies in Jamaica, ya know," said Greg.

Kevin nodded. "Good move. Join us at our table." He waved to Lori to bring the boys a round. "I got that e-mail off to NORAD. We should have the latest on that Air Canada plane by tomorrow."

"As well as a response from his mother on that fish photo. It's my guess she'll think he bought it," joked John. The boys laughed as they took a seat.

"Well, good evening fellas. I heard you guys had some fun today," said Lori, standing beside their table with her warm smile. While she was taking their order, five tall men in snowmobile outfits entered the Lodge and chose a table close to Kevin and John.

Before sitting down, one of the men—heavy-set and tall—put a Loonie on the rail of the pool table to indicate he wanted to play the winner. He slowly eyed Kevin and John's army fatigues. "Well, I hope I don't have to take on both armies to own that table," he said in a loud voice, then laughed as he sat down with his companions, who did not seem to appreciate his humour.

Kevin and John ignored his sarcasm and played their game.

Lori soon returned with their drinks. She spoke to Darren in a quiet voice, keeping her eyes carefully away from the new arrival. "He just got out last week."

Darren nodded. "I know. He's already been banned from The Riverside and The Ironhorse."

"Put that round on our tab," said John from the pool table.

"I'm sorry but this one's on Charley," said Lori.

"Well that's nice of him," said Greg. "Can you thank him for us Lori?"

"You can thank him yourself," she said looking towards the bar.

Greg held up his beer with the others to thank him as Charley waved back with a smile.

Lori made her way over to the other table where the five new customers sat. Kevin could see by the look on her face that she was not comfortable when taking their orders. He scanned the men — all eyes were following Lori, some more discreetly than others. Just as Lori turned her back to head away from the table, the loud one reached out and patted her buttocks.

"I think she could be a real handful," he said out loud.

This was too much abuse for Lori. She stopped dead in her tracks and turned around to face the culprit. All eyes in the Lodge were focused on her. "Keep your bloody hands off me!" she warned.

Slowly, the man stood up from his chair, and then grabbed his crotch and smirked. "How'd you like to put some of your lipstick on my dipstick?"

Lori's face flushed, she exhaled slowly, trying to keep her cool.

Kevin couldn't watch Lori take any more abuse from this sick animal. "I think you should just sit back down and keep that big mouth of yours shut," he said calmly, as he took a shot on the pool table.

The tall, burly man's eyes widened. He made his way towards the pool table and stopped just a couple of feet from Kevin, staring him down. The man's voice intensified. "Do you have a fucking craving for hospital food?"

Kevin didn't reply. He calmly chalked his pool cue and studied the table for his next shot.

John stood alert at the end of the table, ready for anything.

Kevin's actions infuriated the goon as he grabbed Kevin's cue firmly with his left hand.

Lori was frightened for what harm might come to Kevin. "Get the hell out of here right now before I call the police!" she yelled.

Kevin arched his eyebrows and grinned up at the thug. "I think you should take the lady's advice and get going while the going's good."

"Oh yeah?" said the thug as he quickly swung his right fist around to sucker-punch the left side of Kevin's head.

Kevin brought up his left hand with lightning speed and caught the thug's fist like a baseball. He bent the man's wrist back and kicked his legs out from under him, sending the big man down hard on his back, screaming in agony. Kevin kept tension to the man's bent wrist. Everyone watched as Kevin took the bottom end of his cue and pressed it down hard on the man's neck. The man squirmed like a worm on a hook as beads of sweat rolled off his forehead.

"Now, will you take the lady's advice and get your big fat ass out of here?" asked Kevin in a calm voice as he applied a little more pressure to the thug's wrist.

The man nodded his head slowly, looking up at Kevin. "Yes. Please don't break it," he whimpered.

"Very good," said Kevin. "But before I let you leave I want you to apologize to the lady."

The man took a deep breath as his eyes made their way over to Lori. "I'm sorry," he whimpered like a child.

Kevin lifted his cue and let go of the culprit's wrist then took one step backward, positioning himself sideways. Everyone watched the big guy slowly get up off the floor while favouring his wrist. He made his way towards the main entrance where he struggled to zip up his parka. He stopped at the doorway and pointed back at Kevin as he opened the door. "You're fuckin' dead," he shouted.

"That's it! I'm calling the police," said Lori as she rushed towards the bar.

"Fuck you, bitch!" he shouted as he slammed the door behind himself. Not a word was spoken until the sound of his snowmobile engine could be heard.

"Thank god someone put him in his spot," muttered a customer, breaking the silence.

"We're sorry for the crap that asshole caused. He followed us in from Iron Bridge," said one of the four men that the culprit had entered with.

"Hell, no problem," said Kevin. "He is just a lost puppy, desperately trying to impress whoever he can."

Darren stood up from his chair and looked out onto the darkened lake where a single sled light headed in a northeasterly direction. "It looks like Brutal Bruce is headed over to Elliot Lake."

"Yeah, he feels a little tougher around seniors," laughed Greg.

Lori approached Kevin and John with a big smile and two bottles of beer on a tray. "This is from Charley for being the first one to put the run on that bastard."

"Yep," said Greg holding his beer up high. "The last time I ever saw moves like Kevin's was from Steven Segal!"

"Right on," said Darren as he too held up his beer bottle.

# CHAPTER 20

Later that evening, Kevin and John retired to their cabin. a little buzzed from all the beers they had consumed.

"So you mean to tell me that you *learned* those fancy-dancey moves back in Boot Camp?"

Kevin looked up at John as he opened his laptop. "Well, all except for that pool cue manoeuver. I figured it made for a good prop."

"Well, you sure as hell entertained the locals. We never had to buy a beer all freakin' night."

"Yeah, they probably enjoyed hearing that bad ass cry like a baby," said Kevin as he checked his e-mails.

John grabbed two beers from the fridge and made his way over to join Kevin. "Well,

I hope I can figure out what the hell went wrong with our meteor coordinates."

Kevin broke out in laughter. "Here's a reply from my ma. '*Nice catch son. I hope you're eating well*...blah...blah...blah... *Hope you keep watch over your shoulder at all times for them there polar bears. Have a great holiday up in the north'*...and then she says she's in a hurry to attend my Uncle Mike's retirement party." Hmm...he's retiring," Kevin muttered to himself as he grabbed another beer.

"What's he retiring from?"

"The U.S. Air Force," said Kevin in a casual tone.

"How many years of service did he have?"

Kevin took a swig from his beer. "Close to forty."

"Forty years' service? What was his rank?"

Kevin's face suddenly tightened.

"What? What is it?" asked John.

"It's a reply I got back from Roger about that Air Canada flight. You're gonna have to check this out."

John stood up from his chair and made

his way over to Kevin. After reading the first two lines from the report John's eyes widened. "What? No radio communication with Toronto Control Centre or NORAD after having eight feet from one of its wing tips sliced clean off!?"

Kevin nodded. "It wasn't until they got close to the Sudbury Airport that they could communicate. They couldn't send out a mayday or a 7600 alert. As for whatever sliced off the wing, it's still a mystery. It's under top-secret investigation. Terrorism hasn't been ruled out."

"Do you think they're waiting for someone or some group to claim responsibility?" asked John.

"It's quite likely." Kevin continued to scroll down.

"The story sure is a lot different than what Greg heard on the radio," said John.

"Are you kidding? The media is just getting the runaround. But that could be good; the people won't panic in this situation until they know for sure." Kevin kept scrolling. "Check this out John...it was traveling from Montreal to Vancouver at 35,000 feet. The flight recorder's time of impact was

9:14 P.M. NORAD's satellite tracked their U.T.M coordinates to zone 17, E352584 and N5140588." Kevin's eyes were still glued to his monitor. He minimized his e-mail and found a map of Northern Ontario on the Web.

His gasp broke the silence. "Shit, that's *impossible*! The coordinates of the meteorite are almost identical to the ones recorded from the Air Canada flight. Fuck!"

John's eyes widened as he came over to stare at the screen. "Goddamn right, it's fuckin' weird!"

Kevin slowly looked up at John. "This is a freakin' nightmare. How is it possible that those two coordinates are so god damn close to each other?"

John raised his hands in disbelief. "NORAD's track on the Air Canada's 767 mishap is approximately four hundred yards south of our meteor. That puts it somewhere very close to Greg's fishing shack." He arched his brows. "You're not thinking what I'm thinking?"

Kevin looked up at John. "That Greg and J.P. are terrorists? If this is the Taliban's way of reclaiming power, it would certainly demonstrate to other NATO countries how strong their offensive can be in a distant land."

John shook his head. "No Kevin. I'm sorry. I just can't see the Taliban using a Polak and a Frenchie to help them reclaim power. How could they persuade them into working against their own country?"

There was a pause as Kevin stared at the ceiling. "Well, by kidnapping their wives for starters."

John took a deep breath and exhaled slowly. "Oh my god. It's making sense, but it's *unbelievable*. What about Darren and Lori? And let's not forget about that new abandoned fishing shack close to theirs. What gives with that?"

All of John's questions were too much for Kevin to take in. He rubbed his chin. "I did promise Greg that I would show them a printout of the Air Canada mishap but unfortunately I didn't bring my printer."

"Do you suggest we bring your laptop to his hut?"

Kevin shook his head. "Hell no. Once they know we have their coordinates we'll be fish food in the bottom of Matinenda. I'm going to e-mail myself at NORAD all this shit as well as their names just in case things get real crazy."

John looked at Kevin. "How much crazier can this situation get?"

Kevin shrugged. "I mean, in case anything should happen to us at least they would be exposed. We'll join them tomorrow and take them up on that trout dinner. Leave it to me to explain the Air Canada bullshit to Greg. For now, we should just keep our eyes and ears open and play stupid."

# CHAPTER 21

Two provincial police officers chatted as they patrolled the north end of Lake Matinenda. They'd been up since dawn on the routine patrol and so far it had been a quiet morning.

"Sure nice to have our communicators working this morning."

"Yeah, so far so good."

"What do you say we drop by the Lodge for breakfast?"

"You mean you want to check out that hot dish working there."

A snowmobile stopped in the middle of the lake caught the men's eyes. "I wonder what that sledder is up to."

"Probably making a phone call."

As the officers approached, they could make out the frame of a large man. Something seemed not quite right with his posture. His hands gripped the handlebars while he faced forward in an upright position—as if he were driving. Both cops went silent as they parked their sleds.

"Ah shit. I don't like the looks of this," said the one officer as he got off his machine and raised his visor.

"Maybe he's passed out," replied his seated partner.

"I don't think so. He should have heard us pull up. Hey! Buddy! Are you OK? He's not responding," said the officer looking back at his partner.

"Give him a nudge."

"*Hey! Buddy! Are you OK?*" the cop asked aggressively, patting the man on the shoulder. Instantly the man's body and snowmobile parted in half and fell to the ice.

The officer gasped and jumped off to one side.

"Holy *shit*!" yelled his partner.

Shocked, the officer got up from the snow, as he stared down at the man and his sled—sliced clean in half…like two pieces of frozen bread.

# CHAPTER 22

The smell of bacon, sausage and fresh coffee permeated the air as Kevin and John finished up their hearty breakfast at the Lodge. They had just pushed back their plates as Lori came by to top up their coffee mugs.

John excused himself to the men's room, leaving Kevin and Lori by themselves.

"More coffee?"

"Sure," replied Kevin holding out his coffee mug. "So are you busy today?" he asked with a warm smile.

"I thought I would have some free time but I have a snowmobile tour coming in from Wawa." She smiled as she poured the coffee—and gave herself a top up—steam rising from the pot.

Kevin was taken by the distance snowmobilers traveled. "They called from *Wawa*?"

"Yep. They first contacted me from the Wawa Motor Inn. They made it as far as the Water Tower Inn in Sault Ste. Marie last night and should be pulling in here around suppertime. Anyhow, why do you ask?" She gripped her coffee mug with two hands and raised it to her lips as her big blue eyes peered over the mug.

Kevin paused as he stared into her eyes and shrugged casually. "Oh, I just thought ...maybe you would like to do some snowmobiling...or play a little pool or something."

Lori lowered her coffee mug exposing a warm smile to him as she reached out and gently squeezed his hand. "Can I take you up on that snowmobile ride later?" she asked in a soft sexy tone. The warmth from her hand made his pulse race.

The stomping of heavy boots could be heard coming from the main entrance. Lori pulled her hand from Kevin.

"It sure is nippy out there this morning," said old Charley rubbing his hands together in front of the fireplace. He made his way towards the table as John returned from the men's room.

"Time for a coffee, Charley?" asked Lori.

"That sounds great," he said as he sat down at the table.

Charley looked uneasy as he removed his Elmer Fudd hat and scratched his head. "I was just down at the boat launch."

"Oh? What was going on down there?" asked Lori as she filled his mug.

"I was curious to see what an O.P.P cruiser and one of Jessie's flatbed tow trucks were doing down there but by the time these old legs got me down there, the officer was already gone. I did manage to talk to Chris, the tow truck driver."

"Did he pick up a vehicle?" asked Lori.

"No. According to Chris, it was the wreck of a snowmobile."

Lori squinted. "You mean you didn't see it?"

"No, they had it covered with a black tarp and Chris said he was taking it straight to the forensic lab at that Roberta Bondar building in Sault Ste. Marie."

Lori looked across at Kevin and John. "That's wild," she said as she looked back at Charley. "Any ambulance?"

Charley shook his head. "Chris didn't mention one."

Lori frowned. "That's funny, eh? A wrecked sled with no one injured? Chris usually drops into the Riverside after work to catch up on where the fish are biting. If there is a good story about this wrecked sled, believe me, we'll hear about it—Darren will get the scoop and can fill us in tonight."

John nodded. "The advantage of a small town. I hope he makes it to the trout dinner at Greg's later."

"Oh yeah...Big Bob takes over the bar at five. He should be at Greg's shortly after six," said Lori as she picked up the dirty dishes from the table.

Charley looked at Kevin. "Trout dinner? Lucky bums. I'm sure glad to see you guys hit it off. Greg and J.P. are usually quite secretive."

Kevin and John's eyes locked. "Secretive?" asked Kevin, looking back at Charley.

"Oh yeah...big time. When you ask Greg where he caught his big fish he will always say, 'by the mouth'," laughed Charley.

"Oh, OK, got ya," said Kevin, getting up from the table. "I'm sorry Lori but we didn't get a chance to try that lunch you packed for us yesterday. Greg forced us to help him with this huge lasagna that his wife made. We'll get into it today. It's still in my snowmobile."

Lori chuckled. "Well, if you don't have a problem eating a frozen ham and cheese sandwich . . ."

"They should be great toasted on Greg's woodstove," said John, pushing his chair out from the table.

Kevin gazed into Lori's eyes. "Thanks again for a great breakfast. We should be back with Darren for 'last call'."

Lori returned a warm smile, holding a tray of dirty dishes. "I'll be looking forward to that."

# CHAPER 23

That same morning, two young radio astronomers from the SETI Institute in California, sat beside each other, listening to headsets amplified through an array of giant satellite receiver dishes and antennas, sensitive enough to hear the whisper of hydrogen at the edge of the cosmos. The male astronomer let out a noticeable yawn as he slid his headset around his neck and took a sip from his coffee mug.

"Stay up late with the boys?" asked his partner as she too lowered her headset.

"No. It's probably jet lag from that seminar in Chicago."

"Oh? I could have sworn that I saw your dented red Dodge parked at the strip club last night," she said with a smile as she took a drink from her coffee mug.

He knew she had caught him with his hand in the cookie jar. “Yeah. I’ve been meaning to get that fixed,” he replied as he fidgeted with some dials on a monitor. He squinted as he looked sidelong at her. “So what were *you* doing there?”

“Oh, me and the girls were curious...and wanted to check it out. I tried to get your attention, but you were too interested in a hot chick swinging around on a brass pole.”

His face flushed. Just as he brought his mug up to his lips an extremely loud, deep, pulsating sound came over the headsets, so loud that they jerked them off their necks.

“Oh my god!” her eyes widened as she pointed up to a monitor that read, *CANDIDATE SIGNAL DETECTED*.

“The status of the origin is tracking strong on most frequencies,” he said, glancing at different monitors.

“I have its frequency reading at over 6.3264,” she said, shaking her head.

His voice intensified. “Oh boy, it’s a strong sucker, all right. OK. I have it recorded and patched in its coordinates to somewhere in that galaxy named HUDF-

JD2. Check this out," he said, pointing to the monitor. "Its signal track from the beacon intensity is well over a hundred gigs. He let out a deep sigh.

So, what should we do?"

There was a pause. "Call NASA."

# CHAPTER 24

"Another morning in paradise", Kevin declared as he and John parked their sleds at Greg and J.P's fish hut.

"Good morning!" shouted J.P, jigging over an outside hole.

"You didn't catch that monster yet?" chuckled Kevin.

"Not yet!" hollered Greg from the shanty doorway. "But he sure as hell is determined. That crazy Frenchman wanted to take down my clothesline to use as fishing line!"

"Don't listen to dat dere big Polak!" shouted J.P.

Kevin and John laughed as they unfastened their helmets.

"Na, the only excitement we had this morning was seeing an O.P.P. helicopter lift off from the lake," said Greg.

John frowned. "A chopper on the lake...?"

"Come in for a hot toddy before you set your lines and I'll tell you the story."

"Can you check my sucker for me dere?" shouted J.P.

"Yeah, yeah," said Greg as he bent over the hole on the shanty floor and gently grabbed J.P.'s fishing line with his fingertips. "Oh yeah, it's lively," he muttered. Greg went down on his knees and reached under the hollow floor of the fishing hut and pulled up two large, white snowshoe rabbits by their large paws and laid them on the floor. "J.P. checked the snares when he went for a dump earlier. I hope that's OK."

"Oh, no problem," said John, surprised that their snares had actually worked.

"Yeah. J.P. was worried that a fox or an owl would raid your snares."

Kevin nodded. "Well that was sure nice of him."

"Would you boys like me to throw them in with our wild game dinner tonight?" asked Greg as he tucked them back under the hollow floor.

"Sure. Go ahead. Just as long as you don't have to fuss too much," said Kevin, as he took a seat.

Greg pointed down to a large roll of Polish sausage and a block of cheddar cheese on the table. "Go ahead fellas, help yourselves."

Kevin patted his stomach. "No thanks Greg. Lori made us a big breakfast. But we'll take some of those toddies you were offering."

Greg grabbed two coffee mugs off a shelf and handed them to the boys. "Now about that O.P.P. chopper. It was on the lake accompanied by two police snowmobiles."

"Whereabouts?" asked John.

"Between here and Graveyard Narrows. They were parked right on the main trail," said Greg as he poured rum into their mugs.

"Whoa, Whoa! You Canadianized it enough. Leave room for the coffee," said Kevin as he pulled his mug away.

"Yeah...well, we only got a few hundred yards from them when the chopper lifted and headed due west. The two sleds headed in the same direction," said Greg as he added coffee to their rum.

John looked down at Kevin. "I wonder if it has anything to do with that snowmobile wreck that the O.P.P. took off the lake earlier?"

Kevin nodded. "I was thinking the same."

"A snowmobile wreck?" asked Greg.

Kevin looked up at Greg. "Charley said that a flatbed tow truck left the landing boat launch earlier this morning with a wrecked snowmobile. We heard they were sending it to a forensic lab in Sault Ste. Marie."

Greg's face tightened. "Did Charley say what type of sled it was?"

"He didn't see it, it was covered with a tarp."

"Now that really sounds strange," said Greg, "we didn't see anything on the snow to indicate that an accident happened—no blood, no debris. Was there an ambulance?"

"Apparently not, according to Charley," said John.

Greg took a sip from his mug. "Well, we should find out from Darren tonight what all this bullshit is about."

Kevin smirked. "That's funny. Lori said the same thing earlier."

John slapped Kevin's shoulder. "That's why we showed up late this morning. I had to pry lover boy away or they would *still* be talking."

Kevin's face reddened at John's remark. "As *if*."

Greg smiled. "She looked pretty damn good last night...wearing that tight skimpy sweater and jeans. I thought I was going to need a shot of nitro for my heart."

Kevin looked to steer the conversation away from Lori and back to something within his comfort level: the mysteries that seemed to be piling up. "I don't mean to change the subject Greg, but I did get some interesting feedback from NORAD."

There was a pause as John looked at Kevin in wonder. *Did Kevin think it was safe enough to tell Greg this confidential information or was he testing the ice?*

Greg nodded. "That's good because we can't get shit on the radio."

J.P. entered the hut and grabbed a mug.

"Kevin got us the latest on that Air Canada plane," said Greg.

"Yah, well according to our sources, that collision happened in this area."

J.P. squinted. "Here?" he said as he pointed down to the floor.

Kevin pointed up. "No, up there... 35,000 feet up to be exact."

Greg looked down at Kevin. "Do they know what it collided with?"

Kevin took a deep breath. "That's the mystery. Our radar didn't track anything before or after the impact. Eight feet of its wing was sliced clean off like a hot knife through butter."

Suddenly the squeal of the drag of a fishing reel could be heard from outside through the open door.

"Dat's him," said J.P. as he bolted out the door.

"Go get him," chuckled Greg as he and the others headed out onto the ice.

"Oh my god," said John after seeing J.P's thick branch bend in half.

Greg watched J.P free his jigging rod from the thick base of the branch before grabbing his gaff off the hut wall.

"Tabarnak!" hollered J.P. as his line continued to peel off the reel.

Greg could see that there was no stopping this monster as he walked towards J.P. with the gaff dangling from his fingertips. "He's a frisky fucker isn't he?"

"I can't believe dis, me," said J.P. with a nervous smile, watching helplessly, as his fifty-five pound test line was coming to the end of the spool. A loud snap from J.P.'s fishing rod left the men in silent awe.

"I'll put an end to this bullshit!" Greg shouted as he headed towards the shack.

The boys watched curiously as Greg entered the hut. John looked at J.P. "What do you think he's up to?"

J.P. shrugged. "I don't know, me. He had a lot of dem dere hot toddies dis morning. You never can tell what dat big Polak will do when he is like dat."

Kevin shook his head. "My buddies back home in Kentucky will never believe this story."

Seconds later Greg walked out from the shack holding up his gaff hook pierced through a large piece of Polish sausage. The boys watched Greg in bewilderment as he climbed up onto his ATV and started it. "Big bait, big fish!" he shouted as he drove towards them. Greg stopped his ATV in front of J.P.'s hole and handed the gaff over to Kevin. "OK, now clip the ATV's winch hook through the handle of that gaff," he said as he pushed the winch OUT button, freeing up some cable slack from the spool.

The boys suddenly realized what Greg was up to.

J.P. shook his head. "Maudit Polak!," he said with a large grin as he ran towards the ice hut. "I 'ave to 'ave a picture of dat, me!"

John laughed as he brought out his digital camera.

"Is the winch cable in the middle of the hole?" asked Greg.

"You're dead center," said Kevin as he watched the gaff descend into the dark frigid water.

"OK Greg. Give us a big smile for the Real Fishing Show," said John, holding up his camera as a steady humming sound came from the winch.

J.P. handed Greg his coffee mug.

Greg smiled and held up his mug for J.P's picture. "Now this is Real Fishing! Eat your heart out Bob Izumi!"

Kevin held up his hand like a traffic cop when the cable went slack. "OK Greg. You're on the bottom."

Greg frowned as he stopped the winch. He leaned over his handlebars to see the slack cable. “That can’t be,” he said with a puzzled expression as he looked towards the shoreline.

Kevin, confused as to what Greg meant, looked up at J.P.

“It should be a lot deeper dere,” said J.P. as he scanned the shoreline for familiar landmarks.

Greg shrugged. “That winch holds one hundred feet of cable. We troll over this rocky shoal every summer. My depth finder reads this hole at ninety seven feet.” Greg winched in the slack cable a few more feet to get the gaff just off the bottom as he repositioned himself on his seat. “If fishing is a sport, then I’m an athlete! Let’s tease that monster a little. Here fishy-fishy,” he said as he jigged the gaff, with the winch switch, bouncing the steel gaff off the bottom.

The boys laughed it up as they took a few more pictures

Greg was taking a drink from his mug when his ATV jolted hard, spilling his hot drink down his chin and onto his parka.

All the men became momentarily mute in bewilderment.

John pointed down to the winch cable that was now rubbing on the side of the hole. “HOLY FUCK he’s on!” he hollered.

“Then let’s set the hook,” said Greg, clinching his teeth as he compressed the winch button down hard. Suddenly his ATV began bucking like a steer at the Calgary Stampede as Greg held on like a bull rider.

John held up his camera. “This is freakin’ awesome! I’m puttin’ this on video mode.”

Suddenly, Greg’s ATV slammed down hard, pinning his front fenders tight to the tires. The screech of grinding gears came from the winch as the cable began to unwind off the drum.

“That fucker is stripping the gears!” scoffed Greg as he held on helplessly.

There was a loud thud. The ATV jolted back into position as the broken cable descended down the hole.

Greg leaned over his handlebars and peered down the hole. A stream of smoke rose up from his burnt out winch. “*FUUUUCKK…!*”

There was a long pause. No one dared to speak.

J.P. slowly shook his head. "No sir. *Dat* is no fish."

Greg groaned as he looked over at J.P. "*What* then? Some *fuckin'* giant snapping turtle that forgot to hibernate?" He looked across at Kevin and John. "Peter Jones is an old friend of ours from Blind River. He caught a fifty-two pound laker this side of Graveyard Narrows back in 1989. It won the Big Fish contest that year."

John's jaw dropped. "Holy shit. That's some monster."

Greg nodded. "It sure is, but old Pete told us stories of other monsters that just wouldn't come off the bottom and snapped his steel line like butcher's twine. Yeah, they're in here all right."

Kevin sided with J.P., it was a little doubtful that a freshwater fish could be this destructive. Kevin picked up Greg's fallen coffee mug and handed it to him. "The Lodge has one of those Aqua-Vus as one of their prizes for next month's ice fishing derby."

"An 'Aqua-Vu'?" asked J.P., squinting his eyes.

"Yes," said Greg as he put his mug into his ATV's storage compartment. You know.

One of them underwater fishing cameras like the one Jeff uses in his hut near Teacher's Bay."

J.P. nodded. "Well maybe we can use his den?"

"No," said Greg. "I think we should lay low on this."

Kevin nodded. "I'll ask Lori later tonight. Maybe she'll let me purchase that one so we can use it tomorrow morning if Darren won't mind picking up another from that there U-Rental Tackle shop."

John smiled as he patted Kevin's back. "Oh, I'm sure that Lori will cooperate with you!"

Greg nodded with a content grin. "Yeah, then we'll see what in the hell we're playing with down there."

# CHAPTER 25

Retired U.S. Air Force General Mike Mackwood arrived at the waiting room in the White House West Wing just outside the Oval Office. "Good morning," he said with a confident smile to the receptionist sitting behind a large oak antique desk.

The receptionist stood and reached out to shake Mike's hand as she glanced at his guest VIP tag hanging from his neck. "And a good morning to you, sir," she replied, eyeing his casual attire. It was strange to see a General out of uniform. She glanced quickly at her watch. "You're a little early sir. Could I get you a coffee?"

In all his years in service the General had never had the privilege of visiting the Oval Office. Standing on the plush carpeting he gazed at all the antiques and paintings in the West Wing, imagining all the past Presidents who had walked past that very area.

The secretary cleared her throat to get the General's attention.

"Oh, pardon me," said Mike, realizing he had been caught daydreaming. "Sure, I'll have a coffee. One cream, no sugar."

"Make yourself comfortable," she said, indicating a leather chair in front of her desk. "I'll be just a minute."

He sat down in the cozy chair and wondered for a few minutes why the President had requested a retired, over-the-hill Air Force General to attend an emergency meeting in his office.

"Here you go, sir," said the secretary as she set down a round, cardboard coaster with a colorful American eagle presidential seal embossed on it and handed him his coffee.

Mike took a sip from the coffee mug and held it between his hands, not wanting to stain the coaster so that he could take it home as a souvenir.

The secretary noticed this and smiled. "Everyone does that sir. Go ahead and use it. I'll give you a few more for your pocket before you leave."

"Oh, thank you. I was going to give that one to my granddaughter for show and tell."

"Aw, that's thoughtful of you sir, she'll love it. So, how was your flight from Kentucky?"

"I drove."

"You drove?"

Mike chuckled. "Yes *m'am*. After all them years in the Air Force I kind of like to see what this great country looks like from the ground."

"I see your point sir." The phone rang. The receptionist picked it up and spoke quietly, then looked across at Mike as she hung up. "Yes sir, they're ready for you now." She stood and grabbed Mike's mug. "I'll take this for you. Please follow me," she said as she opened the door to the Oval Office.

As Mike entered the office he was impressed by its gently curving walls and arched doorways. A radial pattern of quarter-sawn oak and walnut covered the floor. The elliptical-shaped office featured three large south-facing windows behind the President's desk and a fireplace at the north end of the room. The large colourful Presidential seal of a bald eagle in the center of the office impressed Mike the most.

"Mr. President...General Mackwood," said the receptionist as she placed Mike's coffee down on one of the eagle coasters on the President's huge oak desk. Three other men sat at the desk, their backs to him.

"Mike, I'm sure glad you could make it," said President Hartman, standing up from his desk.

"I'm glad to see you as well," said a familiar voice.

As Mike looked to his right he realized it was Vice-President Scotty Bornman, whom Mike had worked with back in Nevada on Project Arrowhead. "Well this is a surprise," said Mike as he quickly shook his hand.

"And it's good to finally meet you," said the President as he rounded the desk to shake Mike's hand.

"Likewise, Mr. President. "But it's too bad it had to be in Clinton's bedroom!" Mackwood joked.

The President and the others exploded in laughter. President Hartman appreciated Mike's sense of humor, especially when it was about his opposition. The President indicated a tall man in his early forties, with a shaved head, who stood next to Scotty. "This is Jack Henderson. He's the administrator for NASA."

"Good to meet you sir," said Jack as he shook Mike's hand.

The President looked at the next man who was quite muscular and in his early thirties. "And this is Major Curtis Kelly, a commanding officer of the Delta Force."

"Yes sir," he said as he saluted Mike. "We've worked on a couple of missions in the past, sir," said Curtis, shaking Mike's hand.

Mike stared across at Curtis with an uncertain look.

"Oh…it was years ago sir, in the Middle East, on a hostage rescue. I was just a Sergeant then."

The General nodded. "Yes, I remember you now. That mission went over quite well." He turned and looked over at Jack Henderson, "thanks to NASA's space telescopes."

"Thank you sir," said Jack with a content smile. The General's thanks to NASA in front of President Hartman couldn't have been better timing. NASA was in desperate need of more government funding and with the President deploying 30,000 new U.S. troops to Iraq, it would put NASA at the bottom of the food chain for funding. Mike's nod to NASA confirmed to the President how important NASA's part was in aiding his troops with technical support.

President Hartman glanced down at his watch as he walked back to his chair. "Well gentlemen...if you don't mind taking your seats I think we'll call this meeting to order." He nodded to the receptionist, who was standing quietly by the doorway. A large white screen began to lower behind him and the lighting dimmed. The President's face tightened. He looked uneasy as if he had been dreading this moment. He took a deep breath as he looked into the eyes of the men. "Well gentlemen...yesterday the White House was informed by NASA that they received a strong signal from outer space."

There was a long silence.

Mackwood gave the President a mysterious grin as he pointed his index finger to the ceiling. "Do you mean from a communist satellite?"

The President leaned forward and locked eyes with Mike. "I'm afraid not. The signal came in from outer space. It was first reported to us from the SETI Institute."

Mackwood rarely looked confused but now a look of puzzlement slowly crept across his face. He shook his head as if to dispel the thoughts that lay there. "You've already ruled out the Chinese, Russians, or even a terrorist tactic?"

The President nodded his head. "Yes Mike. It gets better." He looked up at a map on the screen behind him. "You men probably caught the news on CNN about that Air Canada 767 passenger jet that had a portion of its wing cut clean off with no trace of any object? Well, according to NORAD officials at the Operations Center in North Bay, Ontario, the aircraft somehow lost radio contact with the control tower in Toronto. NORAD's radar failed to track any unidentified flying object. They didn't receive a mayday until some time later as they tracked its course. Three CF 18

Hornets were sent up to assist but they detected nothing. And now for the icing on the cake...NORAD fed NASA the coordinates of where that plane was, at the time of impact. To get an exact fix on this location NASA used a space telescope from the Earth Observation System to take these high-resolution photos. What you see gentlemen is a frozen-over lake in northern Ontario. Those two rectangular images on the ice are ice fishing shanties. We only picked up activity in the hut on the left. There are some fishermen using it. There has been no activity detected in the shanty on the right for the past forty-eight hours. Now this is where it really gets interesting. When NASA used a heat sensor probe to detect activity in the fishing shanties, it picked up this . . ."

Suddenly the image on the screen changed to a large dark object to the left of the occupied shanty.

"What is it?" asked Mike.

The President shrugged. "That's the problem, Mike. The fact that it exists under the ice in ninety feet of water, on the bottom of a northern Ontario Lake, makes it much more difficult for us to comprehend. Ottawa believes that recent problems with radio transmissions in the area are being caused by this. It could be some kind of electronic beacon put into place by the Russians to aid guidance missiles."

There was a pause as the men focused on the screen.

Mike took a deep breath. "So that's what this meeting is all about?"

The President nodded. "As you men all know, Canada ranks as the world's second largest country in total landmass and is protected under the North American Aerospace Defense Command Region. The Secret Service has reason to believe that some of our space technology could have leaked out into the wrong hands." The President looked back up at the screen. "Canada's Prime Minister, like us, has no idea what in hell we are dealing with under that ice. We need to be involved; not only do we owe them big-time for all their support in Afghanistan, this could be a matter of national security at our end.

"So how do we come into play?" asked Mike.

"Because Project Arrowhead was your baby from the start, it would only be fitting that you should be the one to liaise between Washington and Canada. Besides . . .our mission in Iraq has tapped us out for men and equipment. Arrowhead has what it takes in the event that things get hostile."

Mike felt honoured that the President trusted his discretion. He paused in thought while tapping his thumb on the President's desk. "So you want an old fart like me to come out of retirement and head this team?"

The President nodded gently. "Yes Mike, you are head and shoulders the best man for this mission. Canada's Prime Minister has promised us one hundred percent cooperation from all their federal and provincial offices."

Curtis leaned forward in his chair and made eye contact with Mike. "Yes sir. The Delta Force will be at your beck and call twenty-four-seven."

"That goes for NASA as well," chimed in Jack Henderson.

Mackwood sighed. "OK fellows. Count me in."

"Thank you very much Mike. I assure you, you won't be sorry," said the President with a confident smile as he looked back at the screen.

A new image appeared. It was an airport runway.

"Now if you gentlemen will just bear with me for a moment, I'll show you how we are going to set the stage. The airport you see here is located in a retirement city in northern Ontario called Elliot Lake. It was once the world's largest producer of uranium. After closing all of its mines in the mid 1980s, the air traffic at the airport is next to none, other than water bombers in the summer months. We've set up, in conjunction with the Department of Defense, the Department of Homeland Security, and the Canadian Department of National Defense, a bogus major preparedness exercise, starting tomorrow. That way we can bring in our heavy-weight hardware and personnel and there'll be no hassle while we try to get to the bottom of this."

"The media and the small town politics should eat that up," said the Vice-President.

"So Mike. How do you see us bringing Project Arrowhead onto that airport's tarmac without being tracked by Russian or Chinese spy satellites?" asked Curtis.

The General fell silent for a few seconds as he pondered his options. "I guess we'll just drive it across the Michigan-Ontario border."

"I'm sorry sir," said Curtis. "But you plan on smuggling a top secret space plane through Canada Customs?"

"Are you aware that Arrowhead's wings fold back so it could be transported in a transport trailer?" asked the Vice-President.

"Yes of course I am, sir," said Curtis. "But that still doesn't answer my question of *how* General Mackwood plans on getting it across the border."

"OK," said Mackwood with a big grin. I think you mean my strategy?"

"That's correct sir," said Curtis.

"Do you know that Canadian border guards are not armed?"

"You're bullshitting me!" Curtis chuckled.

"I'm afraid not," replied the Vice-President.

"I find that hard to believe," said Curtis with a doubtful look. "Especially after nabbing those guys in Toronto last year with explosives that were linked to Al-Qaeda. Plus, how is a border guard supposed to deal with a million dollar load of drugs in the trunk of a car? Do they expect drug lords to cooperate? Or are those guards fast enough to dodge bullets from an Uzi?"

The General chuckled. "I hear you Curtis. That's how I plan on getting Arrowhead across the border. We send them an e-mail from the Michigan State Police telling them that known terrorists are armed and dangerous and carrying explosives and are expected to be crossing the bridge over the next twenty-four hours. To really play it up we'll post some troops around our crossing. Within minutes their border guards will abandon their posts like they have done in the past. They will then be replaced by their senior staff officials who will be notified of our plan."

Curtis nodded. "SMART!"

"And that's why we need you Mike," said the President with a content grin.

# CHAPTER 26

A reddish-marbled sun set in the western sky as Kevin and John followed Greg and J.P. along the north shore. The sleds made a sharp right turn as they entered the narrow channel. They swiveled their heads as they took in the serenity of the tall pines that stood along the sides of the steep, rocky shoreline, their long, snow-covered branches giving the channel a tunnel effect. Minutes later they were standing on Greg's porch overlooking the scenic lake below.

"This is some purty view from up here," nodded Kevin.

"God's country at its best, eh," replied John as he snapped a few pictures.

"I'm glad you fellows get it," said Greg, opening his cottage door.

Kevin and John were taken by the fact that Greg's front door was not locked. It said a lot about him and the people who lived in this region.

Greg looked back at J.P. from the doorway. "I'll get that venison roast in the oven if you don't mind lighting the sauna?"

"Sure ting Greg...and I'll clean dem dere rabbits at de same time. Do you have dem?" asked J.P. looking up at Kevin.

Kevin shrugged. "Hell no. John and I checked just before we left the hut. We thought you or Greg had grabbed them."

Greg's eyes narrowed as he removed his boots. "That's strange, they weren't there when I checked. Ah well. Come on in boys and make yourselves at home. Grab yourselves a beer from the fridge," he called over his shoulder as he stoked the stove.

"This is quite the place you have here," said Kevin, admiring the rustic log work as he and John hung up their snowsuits on large wooden dowels that protruded from the log wall.

"Yeah, I skinned every one of them suckers for my father one summer."

John made his way to the fridge. "Sure looks like a lot of sweat and blood."

"You can say that again. Not to mention the sticky pine gum," replied Greg as he turned on the radio. His eyebrows rose as a song came over the air. "Holy shit, we got tunes."

Greg had his roast in the oven and was making some small talk with Kevin and John when J.P. entered the cottage with an armful of firewood. "I tink dat dis should do us for de night," he said as he managed to turn a light switch on with his elbow to add light to the darkening room. "I filled up de generator dere as well," he said as he dropped the load into the wood box.

Greg looked down at his watch as he stood up from the table. "Thanks J.P. It's almost five now. The generator should be good till at least midnight. Let me get you a cold one."

Kevin looked up towards Greg and sighed. "Hell, I'm sorry Greg but we have to get back to the Lodge before it closes. I have to see Lori about that Aqua-Vu."

Greg nodded in acknowledgement as he handed J.P. a beer. "Shit, that's right too."

There was a pause as the men listened to the five o'clock news that came over the radio.

*...A snowmobile accident has claimed the life of a Blind River man. Bruce Walters died late last night after the snowmobile he was driving on Lake Matinenda struck a rock cut. According to Blind River OPP, he was alone at the time.*

'No loss there," Greg said.

J.P. shrugged. "A rock cut?"

*... It has just been announced that the Elliot Lake Airport will play a key role with the Canadian and American Departments of Defense, in cooperation with NORAD and Homeland Security, to conduct a major preparedness exercise starting as early as tomorrow. These exercises are expected to run for two weeks. The public is asked not to be alarmed should they see or hear any low-flying fighter aircraft, as well as military ground forces in the Algoma region. Elliot Lake Mayor, Jim Prentice, was*

*outraged by this last-minute request from the Defense department but was reassured that it was standard procedure for these preparedness exercises.*

*In other news, Blind River Staff Sergeant David Waddell has informed Moose FM that for some unknown reason, the sporadic radio signal interruptions that have been hindering residents of the North Shore has eased somewhat but their investigation into the matter is ongoing. If anyone has any information on this matter they are asked to call Crime Stoppers at 1-800-TIPS. This has been Joe Snider for Moose FM.*

There was a pause in the room. Greg rattled his empty beer bottle on the table and stared up at the radio. "Holy shit! More has happened around here in the last twelve hours than in the last twenty years!"

Kevin shrugged. "Those preparedness exercises from NORAD were not on my laptop this morning."

"Do you tink dat maybe dey are practicing for dem terrorist trets?" asked J.P. as he made his way to the fridge.

Greg smirked. “You mean threats.”

Kevin locked eyes with Greg. “I understood him and he is probably right. It’s about facing and being prepared for the future for any new threat. NORAD uses a network of satellites, ground-based and airborne radar, and jet fighters to detect, intercept and if necessary, engage any air-breathing threat to North America.”

Greg was impressed by Kevin’s knowledge and gave a confident smile. “And I thought it was scary when ventilation systems of U.S. government buildings were at risk from terrorists putting anthrax or other poisons in them.”

“Not exactly,” Kevin frowned. “Canada ranks as the world’s second largest country in total landmass as well as holding seventy-five percent of the world’s fresh water supply.”

Greg arched his brows. “One hell of a fuckin’ big target for terrorists to hit.”

“That’s right,” said John. “What they’re doing at the Elliot Lake Airport is being prepared for the future, for the new threat from those fuckin’ terrorists. Those guys don’t give a shit if they die. They will end up in heaven with six virgins.”

"Hell no," said Kevin. "The last report from our intelligence was that it was getting hard for the Taliban to find a virgin!"

"Oh shit. Don't tell me," said John, holding up his beer bottle. "Maybe the Taliban will use Canadian beer for their next incentive, eh!"

# CHAPTER 27

A faint sound of continuous *blips* could be heard as two seasoned NASA technicians, Denis and Clint, sat side-by-side at the Johnson Space Center's Earth Observation Station in Houston, Texas.

Denis spoke into a small microphone that was clipped to his lab jacket as he peered into a monitor. "It's eighteen hundred hours and the object is now headed northwest, one hundred and twenty degrees, cruising at twenty miles per hour, at ninety feet below the surface." He switched off an audio switch and then swiveled in his chair to face Clint. "I don't get it. We're up to our ass in preparations for the shuttle's June launch and our kiss-ass administrator in Washington puts us on this so-called confidential monitoring job for the Defense department to watch some fuckin' frozen thing under the ice in northern Ontario."

"Well, we could always put in a grievance that it's not our job description," smiled Clint as he took a sip of coffee.

"That's not funny."

"It's not," replied Clint as he put his cup down. "It's the 'same-old, same-old'. You scratch my back and I'll scratch yours. But lately I think it's our back that needs . . ."

The conversation was suddenly interrupted by the sound of a second *blip* that appeared on the monitor.

"What the hell?" said Denis as he quickly turned on a visual button and sat high in his chair. He began to speak into his mike. "It's approximately eighteen-zero-three hours and our heat sensors have just picked up another object. It's on the ice and is traveling almost due north at ninety degrees at fifty-five miles per hour."

Clint was intrigued by this new threat. "Hmm..." he smirked. "I'll get a visual from one of the high-res space telescopes." He quickly keyed in the coordinates while looking up at another monitor. "Shit," he muttered.

"What's wrong?" asked Denis, with his eyes still glued to his monitor.

"All I can make out through the darkness is a single head light, from a small craft that's traveling pretty fast."

There was a brief pause as Denis stared over at Clint's monitor. "Oh, it's probably a civilian on a snowmobile."

The NASA technician tracked the civilian for about five minutes on the monitor. It was after the person exited out from what was indicated as Graveyard Narrows that Clint noticed a change in direction from the object under the ice. His eyes peered intently into Denis's monitor.

As he repositioned himself to the edge of his chair, Denis couldn't help but notice Clint's heavy concentration. Denis glanced sideways at Clint. "Is there something wrong?"

"Is it me or has that object under the ice taken an interest in that snowmobile?"

There was a short pause as Denis took some readings. "No Clint, you aren't imagining it." Denis turned the audio recorder switch back on and started speaking. "The object has now increased its speed to fifty-five miles per hour and has ascended from the bottom and is heading due west, in line with the other object."

A wide, bluish light suddenly appeared under the ice on Clint's visual monitor. Clint's voice intensified. "Check it out! It's freaking glowing!"

Darren was half-way across the north end when he noticed a wide beam of light approaching on his right, unlike a headlight from a snowmobile or an ATV. It had a bluish tint and glowed on the ice. *Perhaps it was Greg's ATV with bulky luggage in his front rack that obstructed his lights.* He slowed his sled down to a crawl.

Denis spoke into his mike. "The object on top of the lake has suddenly slowed down, while the other one is still holding its speed at fifty-five miles per hour and closing in at approximately two hundred yards."

Clint leaned towards Denis and muttered. "I think they're going to rendezvous."

Denis shrugged but failed to comment.

As the bluish light got closer to Darren, he suddenly realized that it was approaching him from beneath the ice. The look of this strange object spooked Darren. He quickly squeezed down on his throttle and bolted.

Clint and Denis watched in bewilderment as the underwater object increased its speed and continued to follow. Clint shook his head. "Holy shit! That object is in pursuit!"

Denis glanced down at his readings. "I'm not sure but it's up to one hundred and ten miles per hour and that civilian is up to ninety-five."

Clint looked sideways at Denis. "So what do you think?"

Denis took a deep breath as he tapped his thumb on the desk. "Well, if you do the math, the smart money is on tailgate Charley but I'll go for the underdog."

Clint nodded slowly in silence.

The drama intensified as the gap between Darren and the object began to close. Darren's mind raced. He glanced down at his side mirror and saw the object gaining. He switched his headlight to high beam and could make out Greg's narrow inlet, about three hundred yards ahead. *Could this inlet be too narrow for that object to enter?* he thought. He checked his mirror and saw that the object was only twenty yards behind him. With the inlet still another two hundred yards away it looked almost impossible for Darren.

He was about fifty yards from the inlet when he glanced down at his mirror. He noticed that for some reason the object had slowed down considerably. Darren was finally gaining. He didn't let off the throttle but kept his speed right into the mouth of the inlet and kept motoring.

Back at NASA, Clint raised his coffee mug up high to Denis. "To the underdog!"

## CHAPTER 28

Kevin held a wet towel over his mouth to cope with the heat from Greg's sauna.

"You're doing pretty good for de first time dere," said J.P. as he threw a dipper of water onto the hot sauna stones.

The steam was too much for John to bear. "That's enough for me," he said, heading for the door.

"I'm right behind you," said Kevin, still holding the towel to his face.

"Grab another beer," hollered Greg. "We'll be out to join you in a minute."

Steam rose from their hot, naked bodies as they stood out on a small deck outside the sauna. John peered down toward the lake under the starlit night. "That's funny, Darren should be here by now." He turned around to face J.P. and Greg who were exiting the sauna and held up his beer bottle to toast. "Well...here's to Kevin's first sauna!"

"And in the winter to boot!" replied Greg, as they toasted. "Hey, I'm sorry you two have to head back after dinner," he continued.

Kevin sighed. "Yeah, if it wasn't for that Aqua-Vu . . ."

John smiled. "That's bullshit. You just want to park your car in Lori's garage."

J.P. took two steps back and squinted as he glanced down at Kevin's midsection. "I don't tink dat Lori would want a Volkswagen parked in her garage dere!" he joked.

John nodded. "If he tried to have his way with Lori she'd have him charged with 'assault with a dead weapon'!"

The men burst out in laughter.

Kevin flushed. "Oh come on now boys, you have to allow for shrinkage out in this freakin' cold."

Greg chuckled. "OK Kevin, we'll allow you a little for that but it's not a stretch limo!"

While the boys were laughing it up John noticed a light approaching out on the lake. "It looks like Darren will be joining us after all, eh."

They watched as Darren drove his sled up towards Greg's cottage faster than normal. He brought it to an abrupt stop, jumped off and dashed up the porch steps into the cottage without even removing his helmet.

Greg looked at the boys with wide eyes. "Holy shit. What's up Darren's ass? We'd better get up there and find out what the hell is going on."

# CHAPTER 29

Greg entered the cottage first as the others followed. The aroma of the venison roast was wafting in the air. At the end of the table Darren sat, his head bowed as he stared down at a bottle of rum.

"It sure as hell smells good in here," said Kevin, trying to break the ice.

Darren continued to stare at the bottle.

The boys took up seats around the table.

Greg looked down at Darren while he pulled out some cola from the fridge. "So Darren, how come so glum?"

Darren slowly raised his head. His voice quivered as he spoke. "There's something out there."

Greg squinted. "Out where?"

"It was a bright light...under the ice. It followed me from this side of Graveyard Narrows to your inlet."

There was a long silence.

Greg rolled his eyes. "Oh for god's sake. Have you been into that wacky tabacky?"

Kevin looked across the table and locked eyes with Greg. "I remember some guys on a snowmobile tour from Michigan talking about one of their buddies seeing the same thing."

John glanced up. "That's right."

"Greg, if I'm wrong," said Darren, "I'll kiss your ass on the Post Office steps in Blind River."

Greg smirked as he grabbed some glasses from the cupboard. "I'll remember you said that."

"No freakin' problem. I'll even give you an hour to get a crowd together."

"So Darren...what can you tell us about this light you saw?" asked Kevin.

"At first I thought it was one of you guys returning from the shack. It was when it got closer that I realized it was under the ice. That freakin' thing scared the shit out of me. I pinned my throttle and booted it."

Greg glanced at Darren as he poured rum into glasses. "Yeah...we saw you. So when did you last see it?"

"It was at the mouth of your inlet. I think it was too big to get through."

J.P. laughed as he handed Darren a glass. "Now you have to hear our fish story dere."

Darren narrowed his eyes. "It's not funny."

J.P. returned an intoxicated smile. "Well needer is ours."

Kevin nodded. "He's right. There's something freaky going on under the ice back at the fishing shack."

"Freaky?" asked Darren.

Kevin nodded. "Yes...like stripping off Greg's winch cable down a fishing hole."

"Greg used his ATV winch to jig with," said John as he took a mouth full of rum and cola.

Darren smiled at Greg. "And you wanted to know what *I* was smoking? After my freaky encounter your story shouldn't surprise me. Oh shit, I almost forgot, did you guys hear about Brutal Bruce's mishap?"

"Huh," Greg smirked. "I don't think anyone would call that delinquent's accident a mishap!"

"That's true," smiled Darren.

J.P. looked confused as he stood up from his chair. "What do you two mean by dat dere?"

Greg chuckled a little then glanced at J.P. "A mishap means an unfortunate accident."

J.P. shook his head as he made his way towards the cupboard. "No sir. I don't tink dat it was a mishap for dat son of a bitch dere."

Greg smiled at J.P.'s remark as he stood from his chair. "We caught the story on the news earlier."

Darren smirked. "Well it gets better. Chris, from Jessie's Towing dropped by the Riverside after dropping off Bruce's sled at the forensic lab in the Soo."

Greg pulled the roast out from the oven. "His sled was delivered to a forensic lab?"

"That's right. Old Charley mentioned that at breakfast," said Kevin.

"But did he mention the condition Bruce's sled was in?" asked Darren as he sipped his rum.

Kevin paused for a second. "Come to think of it, no, all he said was that it was covered with a tarp."

"Oh it was strange all right," said Darren. "Chris said that it was sliced clean in half from front to back like it was done by a cutting torch."

Greg scoffed. "That's bullshit. J.P. and I saw his body being air-lifted out and there were no sharp rocks protruding out from the ice or along that whole fucking shoreline."

"Hey, no need to get upset with me. I'm just the messenger."

Kevin looked across at Greg. "Was it an air ambulance 'copter that picked up the body?"

"No. It was OPP," said Greg as he took the cover off the roasting pan.

"Why would they transport his body in their helicopter?" asked Darren scratching his head.

Kevin looked around the table. "Might be that a detective is unsure as to the cause of death or for some reason feels that this case should be kept low-key until the forensic experts have conducted a closer examination of Bruce and his sled. Like Greg said, there are no rocks in that area for him to have struck...and if his sled was cut in half then what about his body?"

"Well, if dat dere son of a bitch's body is cut in half I tink dat dey will bot go to hell," J.P. joked.

The boys laughed as Greg placed a large platter on the table.

Darren leaned ahead on his chair. "So should we keep our stories to ourselves?"

Greg looked down at Darren. "What do you think? You know damn well how small Blind River is. The fact that you work at the Riverside just adds fuel to the fire. All we need is for reporters from CTV or CBC Radio to come snooping around this lake for a story."

Darren could see that he had pushed Greg's buttons and held up his hand in a *stop* position. He looked around the table. "OK, OK...I promise no one will hear of my story or your far-out fish story. I assure you there will be no paparazzi."

Greg's face relaxed as he stared down at Darren. "I expect you to keep your word."

Greg then scanned everyone's eyes around the table. "Remember, from now on, whatever happens at Lake Matinenda stays at Lake Matinenda."

The men's attention moved over to the aroma coming from the huge platter of thickly sliced deer meat and vegetables smothered in thick brown gravy. "My god, we don't eat this good back at our apartment in North Bay," said John.

Greg handed John a large serving spoon and fork. "Well, stop staring and start digging."

Minutes later Kevin glanced up at Greg. "This deer tastes great. Was it shot close to your cottage?"

"No," said Greg. "I'm a member of the Buckeye Hunt Club near Spring Bay on Manitoulin Island."

Kevin looked over at J.P. "You don't hunt?"

"Oh yes. I hunt moose with Greg."

Greg looked across at Kevin with a smirk. "He tried to hunt deer four years ago."

Kevin shrugged. "He 'tried'?"

Greg nudged J.P. with his elbow. "Go ahead, tell Kevin why you don't hunt deer."

J.P. just sat with no comment and ate his dinner.

"J.P. deer hunted with us four years ago on the island. He was stationed in a tree stand on the edge of this farmer's field. He wasn't there an hour when me and a few buddies flushed out a good dozen deer towards him. We heard all kinds of shooting coming from his tree stand but after we arrived there were no deer down. Not one. Not even a blood trail from a graze."

Kevin smiled as he looked at J.P. "So he got buck fever?"

Greg shook his head. "Nope. When we asked why he didn't shoot any he said, 'Dem dere fuckers don't run fair'!"

The boys burst out in laughter.

## CHAPTER 30

Kevin and Darren stood in Greg's doorway, their helmets in hand. Greg chuckled as he patted Kevin's shoulder. "Don't worry. I'll put a barf bucket in front of them party poopers before I turn in."

Kevin looked across at John and J.P. who were passed out on Greg's couch. "I'm sorry for the inconvenience."

"Are you kidding? They're the ones that will have to pay the price tomorrow."

Darren started his sled and looked over at Kevin. "Now remember…just follow my taillight and if something is wrong or you have to talk to me, just flash your high and low beams. And if that freaky light from under the ice reappears we'll head'er back."

Kevin nodded. "Don't worry about me. I'll be right on your ass."

As they departed from Greg's channel Darren and Kevin were tense, anticipating that at any moment they could come upon the mysterious light beneath the ice. Their hearts pounded as they scanned the frozen surface as they flew across the lake. Despite their fears, they arrived at the Lodge without incident.

Darren raised his visor but remained seated. "Well, I'm glad we didn't have to encounter that freakin' light under the ice."

"Hell yeah…I can't imagine how freaky that must have been. Just passing through Graveyard Narrows at night was enough for me."

Darren smiled. "Yeah…things do look a lot spookier in the dark but you did good for a first time night rider."

"Well Darren, let me buy you one for the road…or should I say 'trail'?"

The lights in the Lodge suddenly dimmed. Darren looked down at his watch. "No thanks Kevin. I want to see Big Bob before last call and I have to open tomorrow. But call me if you need anything from town…like that Aqua-Vu from U-Rentals."

Kevin lowered his voice. "Now remember what Greg said."

Darren slid his finger tips across his lips indicating to Kevin that he would keep them zipped as he drove off.

As Kevin entered the Lodge he felt the radiant heat from the fireplace on his face. The lights were dimmed down except for the pool table and the green hanging swags over the bar. A slow mellow tune played on the juke box into the big empty room. *Did Lori or Charley forget to lock the door?* As he turned to exit he heard the distinctive sound of beer bottles clanging together from behind the bar. "Anyone here?"

Lori popped up from behind the bar. "Hi stranger. What brings you to town?" she said with a seductive smile.

Kevin walked towards her. "Oh, I wasn't sure whether you were open for business or not."

"I thought I would be serving you and John for last call so I dimmed the lights so that the locals would think the bar was closed. But when I heard a sled start up again and leave I didn't know what to think."

Kevin smiled as he gazed into Lori's eyes. "I'm sorry for all the confusion. I can see how you got lost in the shuffle."

Lori nodded. "Yes. Big Time."

"Well, John and J.P. are down for the count on Greg's couch. They got a little head start in the rum."

"Isn't that what you men call 'bonding'?"

Kevin laughed. "I suppose you have a point. As for Darren, that was his machine you heard leave. He wanted to make it back to the Riverside for last call to see Big Bob."

Lori looked down at her watch. "He's got lots of time."

"Well I guess I lucked out on the deal," said Kevin as he sat up on a bar stool.

"And how is that?" asked Lori as she pulled out a beer from the fridge.

"I get to have this beautiful barmaid all to myself."

"Oh yeah?" Lori smiled as she handed Kevin a beer. "It depends if you have any more fish stories to share with me."

Kevin raised his brows. "I'm glad you mentioned that. We had some nice hits today that snapped our lines."

Lori pulled out another beer and took a swig. "Sorry Kevin, I'm just preparing myself for a long fish story."

Kevin flushed. "This is no story."

"But you did say you were glad that I mentioned a fish story?" asked Lori.

"Yes...that's right...that Aqua-Vu that you have displayed at the front desk . . ."

"You mean the one we're giving away for the ice fishing derby?"

"Ya, I was wondering...if I bought it off the Lodge for the same price that U-Rental is selling it for, could you replace it with another one?"

Lori slowly nodded. "You mean so you would be able to use it first thing tomorrow morning and not waste half your day driving to town?"

"That's the plan." Kevin took another swig of beer.

"Well I can't see a problem with that. Go ahead and see if it's in good order and I'll lock up."

Kevin checked out the Aqua-Vu and then looked over the manual as Lori stood at his side.

"Now that's different," said Lori as she took a swig from her beer.

Kevin looked up from the manual. "Excuse me?"

"I mean it's strange to see a man actually reading a manual!"

Kevin smiled and continued to read. "Ah frig," Kevin sighed and rolled his eyes.

"What's wrong?"

"A digital video recorder can also be purchased for this unit." Kevin paused for a few seconds in deep thought then looked over at Lori. "If I had a standard RCA cable I could connect it to my digital camera or laptop to record on video. Right now it can only view."

Lori looked down at her watch. "If we get motoring we can make it to the Riverside for a couple and pick up that special cord at the same time."

Kevin shrugged. "The Riverside Tavern sells electronics?"

"No." Lori laughed. "But Janice will be there playing pool until close. She's a good friend and owns an electronics store on Main Street. She'd be more than glad to accommodate you after the bar closes."

"Are you sure you'll be able to run the kitchen in the morning?"

"Thanks for being so considerate," Lori

said as she scanned around the room. "But I think you're my only customer."

Kevin looked deep into Lori's eyes and gently squeezed her hand. "I really appreciate what you're doing for me."

"Don't mention it. Just bring that fish camera to your cabin and pick me up in the visitor's parking in ten."

Kevin looked doubtful. "You'll be ready in only ten minutes?"

"Uh, ya," said Lori with a smirk. "Trust me. I'll be good to go in ten."

Kevin picked up the Aqua-Vu and made his way to the door. "All right. See you in ten."

Exactly ten minutes later Lori climbed up into Kevin's Jeep.

Kevin nodded as he checked his watch. "I'm impressed."

"I told you I'd be good to go in ten."

Slowly Kevin eyed her up and down. He was taken by her quick transformation and how hot she looked with her short black down jacket and her tight jeans. Her long blonde hair was rolled and clipped up high. She wore red lipstick on her big lush lips. "Ohhhh ya...you're good to go all right.

You just keep looking better and better."
Kevin put his Jeep in gear and drove off.

Lori was tickled by Kevin's compliment. She gave him a warm smile and gently patted his hand on the stick shift. "You know that compliments will get you everywhere."

## CHAPTER 31

It was almost midnight at the Johnson Space Centre. Technicians Denis and Clint leaned back in their chairs, coffees in hand.

Denis slowly shook his head as he looked up at his monitor. "This is almost as much fun as watching grass grow. It hasn't moved since it returned from pursuing that snowmobile over five hours ago."

Clint yawned. "Yeah...seems to favour that spot up close to those two fishing shanties."

Denis's eyes narrowed and looked towards Clint. "Are they sure that they're in fact ice fishing shanties?"

"Well Denis, the latest updated site map that we forwarded Washington showed ice fishermen standing over their holes on the close-range ground track we did."

Denis nodded. "True. But it's the one on the right that I think the Defense Department should be interested in. We haven't seen any action from that building since we started monitoring."

Clint smirked. He felt his partner was getting in too deep. "Denis...our job is only to monitor and record their movements. The rest is Washington's baby."

Denis nodded. "You're right."

Clint glanced up at a clock. "Take a break Denis and switch over to the land down under space telescope. It's three P.M. in Australia and I'm sure you'll track some great eye candy on one of their beaches."

Denis looked over at Clint and chuckled. "You fucker...and all this time you had me believing you were tracking for great white sharks!"

## CHAPTER 32

Shortly after midnight Kevin and Lori entered Blind River. "It sure is darn funny how life has its twists and turns," chuckled Kevin.

Lori looked across at Kevin. "Care to elaborate?"

"Two years ago, I was training in a desert at Fort Irwin, in California and now I find myself in a small northern Ontario town in the middle of winter with a hot-looking lady in search of an RCA cord."

Lori laughed. "That *is* funny. So what kind of training did you do there?"

"Advanced training in hand-to-hand weapons and explosives. The army put us through mock scenarios in and around a mock Iraqi village out in the desert to test our ability to spot trouble before it happens."

"Hmmm...that sounds really interesting."

"That's for sure. To make it look more authentic they even had Iraqi Americans dress up like Iraqi civilians."

"So what would you say would be a soldier's biggest threat in Iraq?"

Kevin paused for a few seconds as he tapped his thumbs on the steering wheel. *That was a good question.* "Apart from insurgents armed with AK47s and shoulder-held rocket launchers, it would have to be IEDs"

"IEDs?" Lori asked with a confused look.

"Oh my god, sorry, I should have said, 'improvised explosive devices', you know, things like roadside bombs. They've been taking their toll on a lot of our troops over there as well."

"So you were one of the lucky ones to be able to transfer out?"

"Yep...never did get a chance to use any of my skills."

"Well you sure as hell gave us a good sample the other night with that bad-ass Bruce." Lori pointed. "Oh, hey, that's the Riverside just ahead on the right at that green sign."

"It looks pretty busy," said Kevin as he pulled into the parking lot.

Lori re-adjusted Kevin's rearview mirror and checked out her lipstick. "You should be able to find a spot around back."

The sound of music and people chatting and laughing could be heard from the parking lot in the bone-chilling night, as Kevin and Lori walked briskly toward the rear entrance. Kevin kept close behind Lori as they entered the tavern. The door hadn't even closed behind Kevin when Lori went over to a tall, attractive girl with long brown hair, who was standing alongside a pool table, beer in one hand, pool cue in the other.

"Are you guys lost?" shouted Darren over the music weaving his way through a few people, his own pool cue in hand.

Lori's eyes widened. "So Darren, I'm surprised you didn't stop in for a drink on your way back from Greg's."

"Yeah, I'm sorry Lori but I had enough at Greg's."

"Janice," said Lori, as she turned around, "I'd like you to meet Kevin."

Janice stepped toward Kevin with her hand out, "I've only heard good things about you."

Kevin grinned. "You have?"

"Yes...The way you handled that asshole Bruce back at the Lodge . . ."

Kevin blushed. "Oh...I just gave him a warning."

"Well that's more than anyone ever did to him in his living life!" She laid her cue down on the table. "Hey, let me buy you two a drink at the bar."

Kevin looked across at Darren, feeling guilty for crashing his game with Janice. "So Darren...you gonna join us?"

"Na...sorry Kevin. I have to open tomorrow, but it's only for a few hours so I should see you up at the shanty around two or so."

"That's great. Hopefully we should have a fishing show for you to watch...that's if I can hunt down an RCA cord."

"An RCA cord?" asked Janice.

"Yes. I desperately need one for early tomorrow morning to record from an Aqua-Vu."

Janice stepped toward Kevin and put her arm around his waist and spoke in a seductive voice. "I should be able to accommodate you big boy. How bad do ya want it?"

Lori laughed at Janice's come-on to Kevin. Lori and Janice had knew each other well; there was much between them that didn't have to be spoken. Lori put her arm around Kevin's waist as the three made their way towards the bar. Kevin showed no signs of resistance between these two beautiful women. Darren shook his head, with a big smirk, knowing full well that it would be a late night for Kevin and the girls.

As the three made their way to the bar, some of Lori's friends waved and shouted hello from distant tables.

"Boy...some guys have all the luck," said a big burly man from behind the bar.

"...and some guys do nothing but complain . . .," sang Lori in her beautiful voice.

Janice looked across at Lori. "Isn't that a Rod Stewart song?"

The big man nodded. "Yes Janice, but it sounds a lot better coming from Lori."

Lori reached over the bar and pinched Big Bob's cheek. "Oh...you're so sweet!"

"So how did you escape from Charley?"

"A tour cancelled out," said Lori. "Bob ... this is Kevin. Kevin is a guest at the Lodge.

"Pleased to meet you," said Bob as he reached over the bar to shake Kevin's hand. He noticed the United States Army logo on Kevin's coat. "So you're the one they're talking about."

"I am?" said Kevin with a confused smile.

"Yes. You kicked that big bastard's ass at the Lodge the other night. Let me buy you and the ladies a cold one."

Janice looked up at Kevin with a warm smile. "I first heard about that incident from some of the customers in my store. Apparently you handled that son of a bitch like a baby."

"That he did," said Lori as she rubbed Kevin's shoulder.

Bob glanced across at Kevin as he placed two Coors Lights on the bar. "So, what's your poison?"

"I'll have the same thank you."

Lori looked across at Bob. "Could you look after Kevin while we ladies powder our noses?"

Bob smirked. "Look after him? Hell, I might hire him as a bouncer." He chuckled as the girls left.

Kevin held out his bottle. "Thanks again for the beer."

"Don't mention it. If Sergeant Brooks were here you wouldn't have to pay for a single drink all night and the OPP would even drive you back to the Lodge."

Kevin grinned. "You're kidding."

Bob leaned forward resting his arm on the bar. "Did you know that fuckin' asshole Bruce had assaulted three OPP officers back in Iron Bridge less than two hours before you dealt with him?"

Kevin shrugged. "This is news to me. Was it bad?"

Bob smirked. "That depends on what you call bad. Two officers are still in the hospital on life support and the other one has six broken ribs and his jaw wired. That's why they didn't go up to the Lodge to question you. They wanted his ass for assault causing bodily harm to three of their fellow officers. To them you're a hero. That's why they put his suspicious death on the back burner."

"Suspicious death?" asked Kevin in a low tone. "Hell, I thought he drove his sled into a rock cut or something like that." Kevin was hoping to pump more out from Bob.

Bob took a deep breath and slowly shook his head with a confident smile. "No. That's what the press thinks. That bastard and his sled were sliced clean in half."

Kevin whispered. "What do you mean, '*clean in half*'?"

"Like a hot knife through butter was how Sergeant Brooks described it. And it's got their forensic biologist and technicians totally bewildered."

Kevin's mind was in a swirl as Bob served other customers. *Darren's story on the suspicious death was pretty close to Bob's.*

After serving the customers Bob glanced at Kevin. "So...Darren told me that you and your partner hit it off with Greg and J.P."

"Yep, they're quite the pair."

"Yeah...next to old Pete Jones they've taken their share of monsters from that lake and have some pretty good stories to tell."

Kevin spoke carefully as he gazed around the tavern. "Yeah, we pulled out a few nice ones."

A curly-haired man with glasses suddenly appeared behind the bar. He squeezed his way behind Bob and dropped some empty beer bottles into a case. Bob tapped him on the shoulder. "Derek…this is Kevin. He's visiting us from the Lodge."

"Nice to meet you…I'm Bob's brother," he said as he reached over the bar for a quick handshake.

"Lori tells me that there is a lot of history here."

"Sure is," said Derek as he piled beers on a tray. "This tavern has survived through the Great Depression."

Kevin nodded as he scanned the room. "I wonder what they did during prohibition."

Derek looked over at Bob. "I think Mom mentioned that it was a rooming house and an ice cream parlor."

"Oh yeah…let me guess. Their special of the day was always Rum and Raisin!" said Lori, returning to the bar with Janice.

Derek rolled his eyes and shook his head. "Always a smart ass!" He chuckled as he made his way out with his tray of beer.

# CHAPTER 33

At 3 A.M. the snow was falling heavily. Lori drunkenly hummed away to a song as Kevin struggled to get her intoxicated dead-weight body through the cabin door, then performed a balancing act as he removed his boots. The warmth from the cabin felt inviting as he carried Lori across a large oval rug. He stopped between the two beds and considered his next steps. He had a strong attraction to Lori and her actions seemed to indicate the feeling was mutual. Her easy-going nature took any edge off the situation but Kevin wanted to be certain that she was not influenced by alcohol. He felt that to be intimate with her now would be wrong.

His eyes caught a flashing e-mail icon on his laptop that sat on a small desk between the beds. He looked down into Lori's groggy eyes with a partial smile, as she continued to hum. "Sorry, I don't know where your cabin is." He lay her limber body down onto John's bed and began to remove her boots.

"You're so nice," she whispered, with her eyes half open, as she began to unzip her jacket.

Kevin slid his hand between her shoulder blades to prop her up as he removed her hair clip and gently laid her head back. She looked beautiful to Kevin, this woman he had become attracted to, lying there with her long blonde hair flared out on the pillow.

Despite her intoxication, she seemed to have the presence of mind to reach down, unbutton her jeans and slowly pull down her zipper.

Kevin was unsure whether to help or not. He watched her jeans move down past her shapely hips, exposing a light blue shear thong inches from his face. That sent him into ecstasy. He decided then to help her. He slid her jeans over her ankles then dropped them down beside the bed.

Next, she began to slowly unbutton her low-cut cardigan. Kevin's heart pounded and his cock began to swell. His eyes caught sight of one of her huge, erect nipples protruding out from her half-unbuttoned cardigan. Suddenly her fingers stopped and her eyes closed as she fell into a deep sleep.

Kevin was mesmerized as he stared down at her beautiful body. Was she being submissive, as a cue for him to move forward? To hold himself back from her he knew he had to quickly shift his willpower into high gear. He reached down and pulled the blanket over her while taking one last glimpse.

Still burning with desire, Kevin knew that by checking his e-mails he could dull his craving for her and get her off his mind. He sat down in front of his laptop and shifted his eyes to his monitor. His first e-mail was from his mother. He took a deep breath after reading the subject line: *Is your uncle Mike stationed close to you*? Mike was his mother's older brother. According to his mother's sister-in-law, the President had suddenly taken his uncle out of retirement in order to head a special task force to terminate a terrorist cell believed to be operating in a remote region in northern Ontario. Apparently his uncle would be heavily rewarded after he completed this mission. Her message reported that Mike would be heading the mission from a control centre at the Elliot Lake Airport and she wondered if this city was close to Kevin. Maybe the two could meet for dinner or something?

Kevin stared down at the floor in bewilderment. What were the odds? Did his mother tell her sister-in-law where he was?

He scrolled down to his next e-mail. It was from a fellow American officer from NORAD, in North Bay. The heading read: *You're missing all the fun!*

Kevin's eyes scanned down to the body of the e-mail:

*Hey Kevin! You sure as hell picked your holidays at the right time. You probably heard in the news about our exercises with Homeland Security at the Elliot Lake Airport. In addition to this they put our department on high alert. They even have CF-18 fighter jets on guard at the base in Winnipeg. We are up to our*

*ass with a lot of big brass constantly looking over our shoulders. Hell, you can't even go for a crap without checking behind you. It hasn't been this crazy since 9-11. Personally, I think that this is more than a terrorist exercise drill especially when they altered our protocol. I think they're feeding us a lot of bullshit. I'm going to e-mail Jeff at Cheyenne Mountain to see if any of this shit is happening there. Bye for now. I'll keep you in the loop.*
*P.S. Good luck fishing,*
*Your buddy Clarence.*

All this was too much for Kevin to wrap his head around at this late hour. He knew he should call it a night. Standing up from his chair he stretched his arms out and yawned. He looked down at Lori lying there so peacefully and innocent, unaware of all the chaos going on around her and wondered how long it would be before he could fill her in on what was happening and why he was there.

## CHAPTER 34

Shortly after 8 A.M. at the Johnson Space Centre, Denis casually sat back in his chair, his feet up on his desk, desperately trying to keep his groggy eyes focused on the monitor.

"Hang in there buddy. Our shift will be over soon," said his partner Clint, as he placed a fresh cup of coffee down in front of Denis. "Did I miss anything?"

Denis reached for his cup. "Oh yeah, it was so exciting I almost fell asleep."

Clint looked down at Denis with a canny smile. "Well then maybe we should switch back to our telescope over Australia to the sun-tanning twins in their dental floss bikinis."

"No, I don't think so," smirked Denis as he looked up at the clock and calculated the time difference. "No, they would have left by now."

Clint smirked. "Well, there is always Jamaica or Rio."

A smile grew on Denis' face as he took his feet off his desk and began keying in some coordinates on his keyboard. An image suddenly appeared on one of the monitors of a beach in South America. Girls were playing beach volleyball. "Oh yeah, now that's what I call a spectator sport!"

The two men had just started to get into the game when two red blips appeared on the main monitor. Clint sighed. "Shit, that's just great. We have to stop for a message from one of our sponsors."

Denis shifted to the edge of his chair as he intensely watched the flashing dots move across the monitor. He glanced sideways at Clint. "Quick! Switch over to our space telescope on that monitor so we can get a visual." Seconds later, a white image flashed up on the monitor. "What's wrong?" asked Denis in a frantic voice.

Clint shrugged. "Beats me...just a sec." He quickly keyed in something on his keyboard. A few moments later a satellite weather map appeared, showing a large snow belt covering the area they were monitoring. "Go figure," said Clint shaking his head.

"What's wrong?"

"So much for our visual from our space telescope. From this map it looks like most of northern Ontario and Michigan will be clouded in for some time."

"Well Clint, according to the heat sensors, those two objects entered onto Matinenda from Big Moon Lake."

Clint nodded. "Ya, it's probably two snowmobiles. Looks like they're headed due west towards those two fishing shanties."

Just then, three more dots appeared on the monitor. These were traveling from the west end of the lake heading east. Clint frowned. "Hmm...that's strange."

There was a pause. Denis squinted as he looked over at Clint. "What in the hell do you think is going on?"

Clint shrugged. "The hell if I know. Maybe they're going to rendezvous or something."

# CHAPTER 35

After exiting the terrifying ride through Graveyard Narrows, and driving his sled across the north end of Lake Matinenda through a blinding snowfall, Kevin felt only relief as he caught sight of Greg's fishing shack. He also felt a lingering sense of guilt for leaving Lori.

After parking his sled he exchanged waves with J.P. who was out jigging over his hole. He heard a radio playing inside Greg's shack. After removing his helmet he heard the same tune echoing faintly from the shanty to the right. Peering through the heavy snowfall he noticed two sleds parked in front of the other shanty, smoke billowing from its chimney—their neighbours must have finally arrived. Kevin looked over at J.P. A thick layer of snow had caked on the top of his beaver-skin hat indicating he'd been there for awhile.

"Any luck?" Kevin shouted over the wail of the wind as he unfastened a large duffle bag from his sled.

J.P. didn't reply. He just shook his head and continued to jig. Kevin was surprised that J.P. was out fishing so early after all the drinking he and John had done the night before.

When Kevin opened the shanty door he was overwhelmed by the aroma of freshly brewed coffee and frying sausage. Greg was on duty at the stove already.

"Good morning!" said Greg, turning from the hot stove.

Kevin smiled when he noticed John hunched over and gazing down into his coffee.

"You can leave the door open," said Greg as he poured Kevin a coffee.

"Are some of ya moving a little slow this morning?" asked Kevin as he laid his duffle bag on the floor.

John didn't reply and continued to stare into his mug.

Greg shrugged as he looked out the window toward J.P. "Huh…that's odd. J.P. isn't that talkative this morning either. I think they're rum-in-iscing!"

Kevin reached down into his bag and pulled out a bottle of Jack Daniels. He unscrewed the top and held it out towards John's coffee mug. "Here you go partner. Bite back the snake that bit ya."

John put his hand over his coffee mug then slowly shook his head.

Greg chuckled from deep within his chest and held out his mug. "Go ahead. We'll bite that snake together."

Kevin topped off their mugs. " I see that your neighbours have finally arrived."

"Oh yeah...I met them earlier. It's two young bucks and their honeys from Elliot Lake."

"Elliot Lake? No shit?"

"That's right. They towed that shack all the way in from the snowmobile trail that follows the hydro line and then they connected onto Big Moon Lake that links to here."

Kevin looked confused. "But wouldn't that shack be a little awkward to tow in from that distance?"

Greg shook his head. "They towed it in as a portable then assembled the walls and roof after." He sat down at the table. "Yeah, I remember now having a chat with them when they drove their sleds through here last March. They must have noticed a few large trout that we had laying on the ice and I guess the rest is history. But we don't have to worry about them fishing this lake out," Greg chuckled, "especially since they forgot their ice auger!"

"You're shitting me," replied Kevin as he took a swig from his mug.

Greg smirked. "No shit. They hauled out a big freakin' car battery and a car radio with fancy-ass speakers but forgot their auger! Go figure."

Kevin nodded. "Yeah…I heard it playing outside."

"One of the boys dropped by here earlier and asked to borrow my auger just to drill two holes. I'm not fond of lending out my things to strangers so I went over and drilled the holes for them, one outside, and one inside."

"Well that was mighty neighbourly of ya."

"Up here in the backwoods, we call it The Law of the Land. You always help your fellow man. What goes around comes around."

Kevin nodded. "Hell…my dad always preached that to me."

The sound of loud French expletives came from outside and jolted John to attention. All eyes turned to J.P. as he appeared in the open doorway. He paused for a few seconds and shook his head.

Greg chuckled. "Let me guess. Your buddy was back?"

J.P. looked at the boys with a poker face. "What can I say, me? I'm jigging away and den, in de *middle* of de blue, dat ting hits my line and breaks it just like before."

Kevin and John were excited by J.P.'s fish story, but dared not smile at his mangling of English.

Greg glanced across at J.P. and sat a coffee down for him. "I think you mean, '*out of the blue*'?"

J.P. huffed and rolled his eyes back. "Out of de blue or in de fuckin' blue is all de same for me dere!" he said in an abrupt manner.

Kevin did his best not to grin as he reached down into his bag. "Well J.P., I think you're gonna finally have a chance to see what in hell was stealing them there big sucker minnows of yours."

J.P. watched intently as Kevin pulled out a blue vinyl box that looked like a small TV screen. Kevin placed it on the table with a proud smile. "*This*, my friends, is an Aqua-Vu," he said as he went back down into his bag and pulled out his laptop. "We'll use the laptop as a second monitor as well as a recorder." He reached back into his bag and pulled out a plastic fish painted as a perch. "This is the camera. I reckon its fish design helps it from spooking fish."

Greg nodded. "Smart!"

Kevin tapped the fish mouth with his index finger. "This is the lens. It has adjustable-intensity infrared lighting that maximizes viewing distance in low-light situations, like under this ice."

J.P. sipped his coffee as he tried to take in Kevin's technical lingo.

"We can connect the monitor to the laptop with this small cable. Lori and I had to drive to Blind River for it. We'll be able to view and record on my laptop *and* on the Aqua-Vu monitor."

Greg's eyes narrowed. "So where in god's name did you pick up that cord at that hour of the night? Blind River rolls up their streets after five."

Kevin smiled. "A friend of Lori's owns an electronic store on Main Street. We just happened to meet up with her at the Riverside Tavern."

Greg nodded back with a big smile. "Oh yeah…Janice…she's a real sweetie as well."

Kevin glanced at John and poked him with his elbow. "That she is, and she is going to drive her sled to the Lodge tonight to join us for dinner and a few games of pool."

John's face tightened as he locked eyes with Kevin. "What? Tell me you didn't set me up!"

Kevin shrugged with a big smirk. "Hell, don't look at me John. Lori invited her. But who knows what can happen if you play your cards right!"

John scoffed. "That's just freakin' great…a blind date from Blind River!"

# CHAPTER 36

Inside the fenced-in, high security facility at the Elliot Lake Airport, General Mackwood peered out his office blinds onto the tarmac. Blue flashing lights lit up the night as snow-plows desperately tried to keep the runways open. Feet up on the desk, he savoured a big cigar, while casually making small talk with his wife on speaker-phone.

"So...is it snowing up there?"

"Oh yeah dear...we are up to our asses in the white stuff." Mike chuckled.

"And how's the food?"

"Great...you know, their bacon is better than ours. As for the beer...what can I say? I only had three last night and slept like a baby. I'm enjoying a Cuban cigar as we speak. Only in Canada, eh?"

"I e-mailed Sandy about your mission up there in the north and she e-mailed me back. Apparently Kevin is on a ten-day leave from NORAD, on an ice fishing trip, with a fellow officer. They're lodging north of a small town called Blind River just west of Elliot Lake."

Mackwood's voice intensified. "So why in the hell did you mention my mission to her in the first place? I told you it was top secret."

Mike's wife's voice softened. "Well dear we thought maybe you two could use a little bonding."

Mike didn't like where the conversation was going and took a deep breath. "Darling, you both know why he's stationed in North Bay and we know Kevin's feelings about this situation so I think that you and my sister should give it a rest and let me do the thinking."

The conversation was suddenly interrupted by a loud knocking on the door.

"Honey, I'll call you back later," said Mike as he switched her off his speaker phone and took his boots down from his desk.

"Come in!" he ordered.

Major Kelly swiftly entered Mike's office, stood at attention and saluted.

Mike looked up from his desk. "At ease Kelly. What's the nature of this visit?"

Kelly spoke in a frantic tone. "Your presence is needed in the command centre immediately sir."

Mike shrugged. "Could you elaborate a little?"

Curtis took a deep breath. "Well sir…all I can say is that the tracking technicians are in over their heads with some strange shit, sir."

Mike nodded as he reached for his hat and overcoat. "You're dismissed Kelly. I'll meet you in the command centre in two minutes."

The General entered a large, portable building. It was equipped with a wide array of satellite tracking systems. Mackwood brushed the snow off his hat and coat as he approached the Major and two tracking technicians who were huddled around a monitor.

They jumped to attention at the site of the General.

"What's all the fuss?"

"We don't know sir," replied a technician. "They were first intercepted entering the Earth's orbit by Space Command at the Pentagon."

The General's eyes widened as he stared down at the monitor. "*They*?"

"Yes sir," replied the technician as he pointed down to his radar scope at three dots that sat motionless in the centre of his monitor.

Kelly glanced over his shoulder at Mackwood. "Yes sir. Johnson Space Centre has these three bogies locked in as well."

Mike took a deep breath and paused for a few seconds while he tried to wrap his head around the bizarre development. He glanced across at the technician and scowled. "Tell NORAD to send us their latest tracks and a map of their trajectory as well as their proximity."

The technician swiveled his chair and looked up at the General. "Ah sir…their proximity is approximately ten miles due west of us."

Mackwood's eyes narrowed. "You mean only ten miles west of our location?"

"Yes sir," said the other technician as he pointed his pen at six dots on his monitor. "Because of the heavy snowfall it makes it impossible to get a visual from our space telescopes. But we know that the bogie to the lower left is that object we have been tracking under the ice. The other two are ice fishing shanties. Our heat sensors must be picking up signals from their woodstoves. The other three to the right are the latest attraction. They're hovering above the ice at approximately three hundred feet."

Mike was in a boggle as he stared up at the monitor. This sudden turn of events had caught him off guard. The atmosphere was tense. Three UFOs hovering in a restricted air space only ten miles away, was just a little too close for comfort. He thought of the fighter pilots with the Aerospace Defense Command sitting outside in their F-16 Falcons waiting for the inevitable.

Mike slowly nodded and patted the Major's shoulder. "Kelly, I think it's time for our Falcons to stretch their wings. Mike looked across the room at the fighter duty officer known as the FIDO. He could provide Mike with a complete picture since his job was to track weather patterns and stay in close communication with NORAD's Air Centre. "FIDO!" Mike wailed. "Get ready. We are about to send up a few birds for a little exercise."

FIDO held up his thumb and nodded in acknowledgement.

# CHAPTER 37

Kevin sipped his coffee while he gazed out of the shanty window at the storm.

"You sure as hell get your share of snow in these here parts."

Greg frowned as he stocked the stove. "Yeah but the last eight years or so have been pretty unpredictable. They say it's because of that global warming."

J.P. reached over and threw his paper plate into the stove and began to clear off the table.

Kevin returned the Aqua-Vu to the table.

Greg smiled. "Whaddaya think? Is J.P. anxious to see his friend?"

Kevin held up the fish camera. "I reckon we should attach a short piece of fishing line and hook below this here camera so we can dangle some bait. It may help to lure in J.P.'s buddy."

J.P. nodded in agreement.

The radio suddenly went static, followed by the now-familiar low, spooky sounds.

"Dat bullshit again!" said J.P. as he sprang from his seat and turned it off.

All was quiet as Kevin held up a finger and tilted his head as though he was trying to hear something.

Greg shrugged. "What is it?"

Kevin pointed toward the other hut. "I can't hear their radio."

There was a pause for a few seconds.

Greg smirked. "Well, I guess they hauled out that battery and radio for nothing."

A tune penetrated through the storm.

Kevin smiled. "Cool...Rockstar by Nickelback. Your neighbours must be playing a CD on that car radio."

Suddenly, a thunderous explosion came from overhead, knocking the guys off their seats.

Kevin picked himself up and scrambled out the door with the others close on his heels.

"What in the hell was that?" frantically shouted Greg as beads of coffee ran down his parka.

Kevin peered up into the falling snow. "That, my friend, was a sonic boom," he muttered.

John nodded. "Yep...it's probably from NORAD's fighter jets, out on one of those exercises."

# CHAPTER 38

Minutes after scrambling up three fighter planes, the General sat coiled on the corner of his desk, staring down at his speaker phone.

"That's odd...we haven't heard from the pilots yet," said the Major, seated in front of the General's desk.

"What in the hell is going on up there FIDO?" scowled Mike into the speaker phone.

There was a short pause. "It appears sir, that we've lost radio contact with them."

Mike rubbed the back of his neck; he tried not to think of the earlier Air Canada flight in that same sector. "No radio signal?" he shouted.

"That's correct, sir. Our radio technicians intercepted some kind of wide band transmission signal from that bogie below the ice. We think it's responsible for cutting off all radio communications with our pilots."

The General shook his head. "Do we have a track on our planes?"

"Yes, sir. Our radar is tracking them due west towards Sault Ste. Marie, sir."

Mike took a deep breath of relief. "Has the Soo airport been notified?"

"Yes sir. We're doing that now," replied FIDO.

The General locked eyes with the Major, as he tapped his boot against his desk. "That's all we need: armed fighter jets landing at the Soo airport! The media will have a field day with that one."

Curtis nodded. "I hear ya, sir."

The men were interrupted by a voice from the speaker phone. "Uh sir, are you there?"

"Yes FIDO. Go ahead."

"We just got our radio transmission with the pilots back. We've lost the three bogies over the lake as well as that transmission signal from that one under the ice."

Mike breathed a sigh of relief. "So where are the planes now?"

"I called them back to return to base. They were about to land in the Soo."

"Good call, FIDO," said Mike in a calm tone. "Which direction did those three bogies head off in?"

"Ah, they just disappeared off the scope, sir."

Mike shrugged as he looked down at Curtis. "…'disappeared off the scope'?"

"Yes, sir," replied FIDO.

"OK FIDO, good work. I'll get back to you for a briefing in my office later. Bye for now."

Mike nodded. "They're fucking with us, Curtis. They think they can intimidate us by first slicing off that Air Canada wing tip and then tampering with our communications. That's why we need Arrowhead. With its robotic satellite guidance system they couldn't have pulled off that stunt."

Curtis nodded. "So when can we expect to have it delivered?'

"About forty-eight hours from now. The FBI is setting the stage as we speak."

Curtis squinted. "Oh ya…I remember your plan now. Something to do with alerting their unarmed border guards that known, armed terrorists are heading their way?"

A smile grew on Mike's face. "Yep, Curtis. It'll go something like that."

# CHAPTER 39

Kevin pointed the Aqua-Vu at J.P. while he viewed him on both monitors. "Come on, smile J.P.! You're on Candid Camera."

J.P. flushed and held his hand out flat to block the lens.

"Holy shit, J.P. is intimidated by a freaking plastic fish!"

Greg chuckled.

Kevin grabbed the hook that dangled down from the camera. "We just have to bait her and we're ready for action."

Greg held out an aluminum pie plate, two large Italian sausages left over from breakfast lay in it. "Go ahead and give one a try."

"You reckon?" said Kevin with a doubtful expression.

Greg held out the plate a little further. "Why not? If it was attracted to the garlic scent from my polish sausage on the gaff then it should be turned on by the garlic scent from these Italian sausages."

Kevin nodded and grabbed one off the plate. "Makes sense to me," he said as he pierced the sausage with the large hook.

Greg chuckled at Kevin's contraption while he opened the hatch door on the shanty floor.

"It's show time!" said Kevin as he lowered the camera into the cold, dark hole.

The boys sat quietly, sipping their coffees. Only a song from Nickelback, coming from the neighbouring hut, could be heard faintly over the wail of the wind as they watched Kevin lower the camera into the dark hole.

Kevin glanced over his shoulder at Greg while he slowly unwound the cable. "Go ahead and top up our cups."

Greg reached over the table with the bottle of Jack Daniels. "Come on fellows. We *gotta* toast to Jacques Cousteau's first underwater adventure at Lake Matinenda."

Kevin was getting close to the end of the cable.

"Hold it!" John shouted and threw his hand in the air.

"What is it?"

John shrugged. "I'm not sure. It looked round and metallic."

Kevin took a deep breath as he steadied the cable. "You scared the freakin' shit out of me when you hollered! Now if you guys watch the monitor closely I'll twist this cable to cover a 360-degree area. We just might see that thing again."

"Wow," Greg nodded. "That gravel bottom is nice and clear!"

"Oh my god!" John's voice escalated. "There it is again!"

Greg jolted forward on his chair. "Yes! I can see it! It's round and metallic."

Kevin nodded as he viewed it on his laptop. "Hmm...OK. I'll zoom it in a little more." As he adjusted the zoom, the object became more visible on the monitors revealing countless holes throughout.

Greg tilted his head back and began to chuckle.

J.P. was soon to follow.

Kevin shrugged at John, waiting for them to stop.

Greg stopped laughing and shook his head. "Well I'll be a son of a bitch! That's the stainless steel slush scoop I lost through the hole last March!"

Kevin peered back at the monitor. "Is there something engraved on the handle?"

Greg nodded with a half-smile. "Yes. 'The Big Polak'. It was the retirement gift they gave me back at the mine in Elliot Lake."

Kevin smiled. "If we drill another hole about three feet past that window we should be right on top of it."

# CHAPTER 40

John handed one end of the Aqua-Vu cable through the shanty window to Kevin.

"You guys don't have to go through all this freakin' trouble. It's just a freakin' slush scoop," Greg muttered as he stoked the stove.

Kevin glanced up while he plugged the cable into the Aqua-Vu. "Hell Greg. With all them there holes in that scoop, snagging it with that big hook will be as easy as shooting fish in a barrel."

The weather started to subside. The odd snowflake fell from the grey sky, making the music coming from their neighbour's stereo seem somehow louder.

John carefully turned the cable in the outside hole, J.P. at his side.

"OK John...just a little more to the right," instructed Kevin from his monitor.

The music suddenly increased in volume as the neighbour's shanty door was flung open.

John and J.P. smirked as they watched a young couple stagger out onto the ice and then sit on a snowmobile.

"OK John...now lower it just a tad," said Kevin.

Moans of ecstasy began to wail out from inside the hut, as a Nickelback tune played on.

"*Geez*...it sure would be nice to be young again!" said Greg.

As the rhythmic moans rose to screams, John had trouble concentrating. He began to chuckle from deep inside, which made the cable sway. "I'm sorry Kevin but..." John couldn't get the sentence out and started to laugh out loud.

Kevin grinned. "Someone should tell them to get a room!"

Greg looked a little uneasy. He glanced at J.P. "OK J.P. You give her a try."

J.P., looking confused, pointed towards the other shack. "Her?"

"No! For *fuck's* sake...The cable!"

J.P.'s misunderstanding made John laugh even louder.

The screams of ecstasy finally came to a halt as J.P. patiently turned the cable.

Kevin could finally see the large hook fall into one of the many holes on the slush scoop. "OK J.P. You got her."

J.P. could feel a little resistance from the slush scoop and began to slowly crank up the cable.

"Good work fellas," said Greg as he watched the ascending slush scoop glitter in the camera's light.

Kevin stood and headed out to join the boys.

Greg, concentrating on the screen in the hut, suddenly spat coffee from his mouth and nose, his eyes wide. "Holy SHIT!"

The cable spool was jerked out from J.P.'s hands and became wedged sideways into the hole.

"Son of a bitch!" hollered Greg from the shanty.

John and Kevin watched as J.P. yanked the spool out from the hole and began to crank in the cable. There was no resistance on the cable.

Greg stormed out from the hut then stopped to take a deep breath. "Oh my GOD! You have no idea what the fuck we're dealing with down there! I've never seen anything like it in my life."

J.P. pulled the fish-cam out from the hole and held it up. The large hook and slush scoop were stripped clean off. "Well we know for sure dat it likes dat dere slush scoop."

Kevin rushed towards the hut. "Give me a minute and we'll check out what we're dealing with!"

Nickelback tunes continued to play from the neighbouring hut where the two young couples were inside, oblivious to what was happening.

The boys sat tense, waiting on Kevin as he fidgeted on his laptop. "OK guys, I'll play it back to the last minute." They watched the recording intensely as they saw the hook snag one of the slush scoop holes and then slowly raise it off the bottom. Kevin glanced up at the boys. "Now this is when I left the shack."

Suddenly, out from the dark, a giant mouth with long teeth filled the monitor, and then darted off into the darkness, all within a second.

"Holy shit! Did you see that?" shouted John.

"I saw some big teet dere, but it was too fast for me to see," replied J.P.

"OK…I'll replay it back again, but in slow motion," said Kevin.

Greg nodded at Kevin's suggestion as he sat closer to the monitor. After rewinding it Kevin pushed down on the 'Play' tab. "OK guys…here we go!"

All eyes watched the hook as it slowly snagged the slush scoop. This time they could see a dark shadow approach the camera. A wide pair of compound pearl eyes glowed and then gave way to a huge horrific mouth that displayed rows of long, needle-sharp teeth. It chomped onto the slush scoop, snapping the fishing line from the camera like a thread and then slithered away, the slush scoop handle sticking out from the side of its mouth.

The boys sat, bewildered by the huge mysterious predator.

"Well...so much for that slush scoop," said Greg as he raised his head from the Aqua-Vu and then stared out onto the lake. "You know...if someone were to tell me a story like this, I would tell them that they were fucking cuckoo in the head!"

## CHAPTER 41

General Mackwood sat behind his desk while the Major addressed a Special Task Force. He pointed to an area map projected on a screen.

"This area up here at the north end of Lake Matinenda is our target. Our counter-terrorist unit has located a weapon of mass destruction that lies frozen beneath on the bottom to the left of these fishing shanties. Our satellites have tracked it wandering in different areas but it always settles here. We believe that it's some kind of unmanned mini-sub prototype that Al Qaeda is testing before launching others into our Great Lakes and oceans. The next few photos are a sample of its capabilities and what we're dealing with. This picture is the Air Canada passenger 707 that had to make an emergency landing at Sudbury Airport. It flew over the same quadrant at thirty-five thousand feet. Eight feet of its left wing was sliced clean off. This next picture was taken at the Provincial Forensic lab in Sault Ste. Marie. It's a snowmobile that was sliced in half from front to back and believe me; you don't want to see the driver."

The Major turned off the projector with a remote and smiled while tapping a pointer in his hand. "However, we have a secret weapon of our own. But we have to set the stage for its arrival. The media has been informed that, as of now, this sector has been cordoned off. Homeland Security will be conducting winter ground combat training exercises. The Provincial Police and local Conservation Officers will be assisting us in temporarily shutting down the snowmobile trail system that runs through most of this area and evacuating all ice fishermen and any winter cottagers off the lake."

# CHAPTER 42

John stroked his mustache as they analyzed the image again. "That fucker looked just like that prehistoric shark that was caught in Japan last month!"

Kevin nodded. "Hell yeah...it was in all the news. I think they called it a living fossil."

Greg chimed in. "Ya, I saw that too, it was on the front page of the *National Post*. It died shortly after in a marine park. Those rows of teeth and that eel-like body sure looked like the photo in the paper."

John smirked. "Yeah but didn't they find that one in the ocean?"

Kevin glanced up at John. "Hmm, good point. But don't salmon live in fresh and salt water during their life?"

Greg's eyes met John's. "Last summer my wife and I visited a museum in

Sheguiandah, on Manitoulin Island. They had several specimens of marine fossils that were discovered there...some dating back over 450 million years ago."

John's eyebrows rose. "Holy shit! That's freakin' old!"

"Damn straight. The one fossil that caught my interest was the sea scorpion: it reached up to nine feet in length."

John's face tightened. "Yikes. That just put an end to my skinny dipping."

Kevin smirked. "Don't be an idiot, John. Greg said they dated back millions of years ago."

Greg nodded. "Good point, but scientists claimed that the shark the Japanese caught was thought to have been extinct. And there've been other birds and reptiles, that they've thought were extinct that have popped up in the last few years. So...you never know." Greg reached out towards Kevin's bottle of Jack Daniels. "Do you mind?"

"Hell no...top mine off too."

They were suddenly interrupted by the sound of a snowmobile pulling up to the hut. J.P. stood up from his seat to get a better look as Greg hid the bottle from view. "It's only Darren," J.P. muttered.

There was a lengthy pause. The thought of sharing their horrific discovery with Darren lingered in the air.

Once again, rhythmic moans rose up from the neighbouring shanty.

Darren entered the hut with a big grin. "Well, I didn't see any fish lying on the ice but from the sound of it they're getting all kinds of action next door!"

Greg rolled his eyes. "Oh yeah…tell us about it. That's been going on all freakin morning. It's a LOVE shack, not a fishing shack! I'm just glad our wives aren't here."

J.P. nodded. "Dat's for sure! Greg's wife would drag him over dere for him to learn more tings."

Kevin laughed. "Oh yeah? Does she encourage that sort of thing?"

"Are you kidding," Greg muttered. "She puts Miracle-Gro in my freakin' underwear!"

The boys burst out laughing.

Darren couldn't help but notice the Aqua-Vu sitting on the table. "Hey, did you guys finally get to see J.P.'s monster?"

Greg smirked at Darren and reached for the coffee pot. "We'll give you a sneak preview of it, but first, I think you should have a hot toddy."

Greg's comment intrigued Darren as he sat down at the table.

Darren was all eyes as Kevin pushed 'PLAY'.

"That round object that you see flashing is, or was, my slush scoop we had snagged," said Greg as Darren watched intently.

Darren's eyes widened and his jaw dropped as the creature appeared on the monitor. At the end of the replay he took a deep breath and looked up at the boys. "What in the hell was that?"

Greg shrugged. "Maybe a living fossil?"

Darren shook his head. "It looks more like a living fucking nightmare."

J.P. pointed north. "And dat ting always goes dat way after."

Greg's eyes narrowed as he peered out the shanty window. "It was out at that far hole where that fucker stripped my winch."

"I do remember you commenting on it being shallower than you had expected, said John.

Greg nodded. "That's right. It does seem to favour that spot."

"Hell it would only take us a few minutes to re-set this rig over there," said Kevin.

John shrugged. "But what would we use for bait to attract it?"

A smile grew on Darren's face as he looked over at the leftover sausage on the aluminum pie plate. "Greg used a hunk of Polish sausage as bait before and that aluminum pie plate should attract it like that shiny slush scoop did."

"You have a good point," said Kevin. "It was after we snagged the scoop that it hit."

J.P. stared back at the sausage in the aluminum pie plate. "Maybe we should use da plate and da sausage."

Kevin nodded. "Good thinking, J.P. I wouldn't want that thing chomping down on the camera."

Minutes later J.P. stood outside over the far hole, holding the camera, with the pie plate and sausage dangling on a hook below. Kevin and John set up the Aqua-Vu monitor and the laptop on two plastic pails.

Kevin glanced up at J.P from the laptop monitor. "OK, J.P. Let her down slowly."

Darren, standing to the side, looked down at Kevin and John and smiled. "So are you two rested up for tonight?"

John frowned. 'What do you mean?"

"Well…with the snowmobile trail shut down it's a good opportunity for you two to party late with the girls tonight."

Darren's comment caught the boys by surprise.

"What the fuck are you talking about?" Greg asked.

Darren squinted. "Didn't you hear about it on the news?"

Greg shrugged and shook his head.

"Homeland Security and NORAD have temporarily closed the snowmobile trail for some winter ground combat training.

Greg frowned. "Well, that's news to us. We turned our radio off earlier because of that bullshit interruption."

"I had that this morning too, but only lasted for fifteen minutes or so."

Greg grunted a laugh. "Well if they stay out of my way, I'll stay out of theirs. And if they think they're gonna keep Doug Olson from his trap line, they *will* need an army."

"Are we almost dere?" asked J.P.

Kevin held up a traffic-cop palm. "Whoa... hold it right there J.P. while I adjust the lighting."

Greg and Darren noticed Kevin's face tighten as he stared at his monitor.

"What in the hell?" muttered John, staring into the Aqua-Vu.

"What is it guys?" asked Greg.

Kevin stared directly at Greg. "Have any boats sank or been reported missing on this lake lately?

Greg's brows narrowed as he leaned towards Kevin's laptop. "Let me see what you have there." Seconds later he scratched his head. "I'll be goddamned. It looks like the large hull of an aluminum boat upside down."

Kevin shrugged. "I'm sorry fellows but that's the clearest I can get from this distance."

Greg smiled at J.P. "Could you get me my ice auger? I'll put the camera right on top of that freaking thing."

Minutes later J.P. was lowering the fish-cam down into the new hole. No one spoke as they stared at the monitor in anticipation as yet another Nickelback tune continued to echo through the still cool air.

Kevin saw the object quickly appear on the screen and raised his hand up for J.P. to stop but his timing was too late. The boys flinched as the camera hit hard on top of the object and bounced a few times. J.P. stood over the hole with slack cable in hand.

Greg shook his head. "Did you forget to compensate for the height of the object?"

J.P. nodded apologetically.

Kevin smirked and pointed upward. "It's OK, J.P. Just hoist her up a little. OK. Now hold her right there."

Darren raised his head from the Aqua-Vu screen. "I don't think that's a boat hull. It has no rivets or welded seams and it looks like there's some kind of weird lettering to the right."

"J.P., can you turn that cable just a tad to the right?" asked Kevin. Kevin's eyes widened as the lettering appeared. "Yes Darren. It looks like some kind of Egyptian lettering above that circular port."

"A 'port'?" said Greg.

The port suddenly opened, expelling a bright, amber light. The head of a horrid creature appeared in the porthole then squeezed its way out and slowly slithered toward the camera.

They watched in horror as two more creatures exited from the port and headed off in different directions.

There was an eerie silence as they watched the first creature close in on the camera. Its huge jaw sprung open, displaying long, needle-sharp teeth.

Greg jolted back from the monitor and gasped deeply as the creature clamped down on the sausage and snapped the line, jerking the spool out from J.P.'s hands again and wedging it sideways into the hole.

J.P. hollered out frantically in French. The guys watched in bewilderment as the aquatic nightmare retreated into the port that closed behind it.

J.P. stood with his hands on hips. "Can someone tell me dere what de fuck is going on?"

Greg took a deep breath as he rubbed sweat from his brows. "To be honest with you J.P., I don't fucking know."

Kevin began to dismantle the Aqua-Vu monitor. "I think we should watch the replays in the shack."

Greg glanced over toward the other shanty. "Good move Kevin. We don't want to attract those love-birds from their nest."

All was quiet in the shanty as Greg poured the boys each a straight shot of Jack to calm their nerves while Kevin assembled the monitors.

"This whole fucking thing is blowing my mind," Greg muttered.

Kevin looked uneasy and raised his chin from the monitor. "Greg, John and I first discovered it last month."

There was a pause. The look on Greg's face was one of absolute shock. "What the ...! Did I hear you correctly?"

Kevin leaned ahead and put a reassuring hand on Greg's shoulder. "Last month at NORAD we thought we tracked a meteor that crashed somewhere close to here so we decided to take some time off the base and go on a little ice fishing trip. I'm sure you know the rest of the story. All that ice that's along that ridge must be the result of that spacecraft crashing into the lake in early December."

John looked up at Greg. "We set those snares inside that tree line so we wouldn't look too conspicuous when we were hunting for that meteor."

Greg nodded. "Smart move. But you should really learn how to set a snare right."

"Oh my god," Darren's eyes widened with the realization. "That's probably what followed me under the ice last night. Maybe we should call the police."

Greg exhaled. "I think we should first find out a little more of what the hell we're dealing with down there before going public."

Kevin nodded. "I can't agree with you more. And we can start by reviewing the video."

# CHAPTER 43

Greg watched cheese sandwiches grill on top of the stove as Kevin replayed the astounding images on his laptop.

"OK J.P. Here comes your friend."

"Is dat de one dat breaks all our lines? asked J.P., squeezing his way around John and Darren.

"Ya! And probably the same fucker that stole my scoop," muttered Greg, turning over a sandwich.

J.P.'s eyes widened as he watched the creature squeeze its large head and body out of the much smaller port hole. "How in de hell can he do dat?"

Kevin looked up from his monitor. "They contract their skulls. Mice can do that as well. Their skulls are cartilage that can collapse. They can squeeze their bodies through a hole the size of a dime."

A nervous look grew on J.P.'s face as he glanced down at the open fishing hole behind him. Shivers traveled down his spine. "Fuck dat!" he said, kicking the hatch shut and locking it.

Greg chuckled as he set down a platter of grilled cheese sandwiches.

Kevin's mind reeled back as he reached for a sandwich. "I wonder if those big, frisky critters could have taken those rabbits from under this floor."

There was a short pause.

Greg nodded. "Yeah...and maybe the rest of that lasagna that was left on the table."

Darren looked down at the closed hatch behind him. "Oh fuck, Greg. That's not funny."

An amused grin crossed John's lips. "Do you think it's possible that those freaky things were flying that craft?"

"Na," Greg scoffed as he grabbed a sandwich. "I can't envision one of them Matinenda nightmares in a pilot's seat."

Darren smirked. "Who's to say they're navigating that ship? There could be a higher form of intelligence on board."

"Oh yeah," smiled Greg. "If they are so freakin' intelligent then why don't they cut their way out with a laser beam and fly the hell out?

Kevin shrugged. "Maybe they had mechanical problems. They crashed, remember?"

Greg grinned back at Kevin. "OK, so what gives with them jumbo eels?"

Kevin held up his sandwich. "Maybe they're a source of food for them and they are let out to forage, like farmers letting their cattle graze."

"Pirates carried livestock on their ships as a source of food," John supported.

Darren turned to Kevin with a curious look. "Or those horror shows could be out foraging to feed the higher life forms later."

Greg scowled after swallowing a bite from his sandwich. "How in the hell would they feed their catch back to those so-called intelligent life forms later?"

Darren paused and looked up at Greg. "By regurgitating it back to them, you know, like a mother pelican does to its babies."

Greg looked nauseated as he set down his sandwich. "OK, Darren. I get it. That was too much information!"

Kevin smiled at Greg's reaction. "I'm just sayin'. You call it gross, some call it survival."

After reviewing the video a few more times, a troubled look appeared on Kevin's face as he frantically tapped his index fingers on the sides of his monitor."

"What is it Kevin?" Greg wondered.

"It's funny, after all our speculating, you know, that craft down there could be pilotless like the Phoenix Mars Lander. It may have been sent here to explore…and those creatures could be like guinea pigs. If only we could leave this equipment out there overnight on time-lapse mode, it would show us if and when that ship moves as well as the feeding habits of them there creatures."

Greg gazed out the shanty window. "Ah shit…don't sweat the small stuff Kevin. I'll park this shack over that far hole for you to monitor."

Kevin looked edgy as he glanced at his watch. "So how long would that take?"

A smile grew on John's face. "Don't tell us you're in a hurry to get back to the

Lodge? Fellows, I think Kevin's pussy-whipped," joked John.

Kevin flushed. "What are you talking about?"

Darren turned to Kevin. "Yeah…I thought I saw a fresh set of tracks in the snow this morning, coming from your cabin."

Greg leaned over and tapped Kevin's shoulder. "I just hope you're thinking with the right head young man because if it's got tits or wheels, it will always give you problems."

The boys burst out laughing.

Greg poured coffee into his mug. "Just kidding ya Kevin…I'm sure that your rugged good looks and charisma didn't hurt your popularity with the female audience at the Riverside. I'm sure Darren's cousin enjoyed your companionship."

Kevin stared at Darren. "You're Lori's *cousin*?' he said, fumbling his words.

"Our mothers are sisters. Does that qualify us?"

"Then why didn't you stay and have a cold one with us at the Lodge before heading back to Blind River last night?"

"There was no one there, remember? I thought it would be good for the two of you to be alone. She's been alone since she came back from Toronto...and I know she likes you."

Kevin blushed. "How do you know?"

"Just believe me. I know. You're all she freakin' talks about, and she smiles every time your name is mentioned."

Kevin stepped out from the shanty and shook hands with Greg and J.P. while John and Darren started their sleds. "Thanks again for moving your hut over this hole."

"Don't mention it, and don't worry about your equipment. I'll load the wood stove up to the nuts before we lock up. It'll still be toasty in there by morning. Go and sow your wild oats. Just make sure you're here in the morning to replay your camera for us."

"Come on," hollered John from his sled. "Darren has to make it in to work."

Kevin smiled back at Greg as he fastened his helmet. "Wild oats? Hell, I don't reckon it'll be as wild as that there LOVE shack down yonder!"

# CHAPTER 44

General Mackwood entered the control centre and made his way over to the Major who was staring intensely at a monitor.

"What seems to be the problem Major?"

The Major looked uneasy. He lowered his voice. "I don't like the looks of this sir. Here, take a look."

Peering over Curtis's shoulder, Mike could only see two dots on the screen. "What the hell?"

"They moved their fishing shanty right above that bogie below the ice, shielding it from our heat sensors."

A sudden, dejected look swept across Mackwood's face, as though he dreaded the moment. "Shit, I wish we had Arrowhead here now."

"So what do you recommend we do in the meantime, sir?"

Mike looked down at his watch. "It'll be dark soon. Have a couple of your men pay them a little visit first thing in the morning...and make damn sure they have back-up posted at the east and west of them...it wouldn't hurt to have a few Apache choppers do a little fly-by to intimidate them a little. After their visit I expect a full report on my desk on how they like their toast in the morning!"

A content smile grew on the Major's face. He would finally get the chance to send his impatient Delta Force out for a little exercise.

## CHAPTER 45

In the neighbouring shanty, the young couple took in a breathtaking sunset through their window. Candles flickered as they sipped from stainless steel martini glasses. Tunes from Nickelback continued to play from the car radio they had brought in.

"It's too bad Cory and Sandy didn't stay to enjoy this sunset," said Tara.

Jeff scowled. "If Cory can't take a joke ...fuck him."

"What happened?"

Jeff looked down at the open fishing hole behind him. "When you girls went out for a leak earlier, Cory claims he saw a horrifying head of a fuckin' monster looking up that hole."

Tara looked stunned. "So what was the joke?"

Jeff groaned and looked down at a plastic bag of marijuana Cory had forgotten on the table. "I told him it was either his cheap drugs or his reflection off the fuckin' water."

Tara smiled and shook her head. "You two always get into the craziest arguments."

Jeff set his martini glass down and put his arms around her waist. "Yes Tara, but it worked out in our favour to have this time alone."

She lowered her voice. "That's why I love you. You're so romantic." She leaned forward and laid a passionate kiss on his lips then used her tongue in a way that drove him crazy.

He pulled her firm little body up tight to his...so tight that she could feel him hardening against her..

His breathing got heavier as she reached down with a hand and stroked his crotch. "Well, what have we here?" she said, with a seductive wink.

Jeff slid his hands around her tiny waist and massaged her ass. "I thought it was time we enjoyed the comforts of this cozy shack by ourselves," he said, and began to kiss her neck as she continued to rub him.

"You think of everything don't you?" she murmured.

Jeff cocked his head with an innocent look. "Uh...not all the time."

Tara gazed up. "What do you mean?"

"I forgot to bring protection."

She gave him a reassuring wink. "It's OK. Did listening to Sandy's groaning and moaning excite you?"

"Oh yeah."

Tara smiled. "Well the same goes for me. But you're not getting off that easy."

"What do you mean?"

"I remember reading on the girl's washroom wall...something about a guy by the name of Jeff, having a fantastic tongue."

"You're bullshitting?"

Tara sat on the wood storage box and leaned back on her elbows and gave a seductive smile. "No...but would you like a chance to defend that title?"

"Is this what they call, 'friends with benefits'? He got down on his knees. He lowered his eyes and reached out to unbutton her jeans.

She knew he was ravenous for her and she felt the same as she propped her butt up to assist him.

In no time he had her jeans off and began to fondle her through her sheer thong.

Tilting her head back, she grabbed the corners of the firewood box, closed her eyes and concentrated.

Jeff felt she deserved satisfaction more than he did. He slid her thong to one side and lowered his face and began to slowly lick.

Thrilled by this sensation, the excitement escalated. Within seconds, a quiet moan escaped from Tara, which blended in with the music on the stereo. After minutes of stimulation, Tara was reaching the point of no return; she opened her eyes, grabbed the back of Jeff's neck and raised her head while moaning out load. Movement behind Jeff caught her attention, what she saw made her freeze. Rising up from the fishing hole, only two feet behind Jeff, was a horrifying creature from hell.

It stared down at them, jaws wide open revealing long, needle-sharp teeth, with dripping greenish slime. Tara let out a strangled cry and tried to push Jeff away.

Jeff felt himself getting harder and harder, *That's my girl, enjoy the sweet release*. He resisted her by grabbing her butt and pulling her in tightly.

Tara froze and began to hyperventilate. Suddenly everything seemed to be in slow motion while she struggled. She watched the creature cock its head back like a king cobra and lunge forward, sinking its long, razor teeth into the centre of Jeff's back.

Jeff was confused by the hard blow. He screamed out in pain as the razor-sharp teeth severed his spinal nerves. He felt himself being pulled backwards. Struggling to look behind him, he saw a large eel-like thing protruding from the fishing hole and fastened to his back. He tried to stand but slipped back down into a pool of his own blood.

Tara watched in silent horror, one hand over her mouth, unable to move.

Jeff's eyes caught a glimpse of a hatchet that was leaning against the wood box. After struggling for a few more seconds he managed to grasp the hatchet handle and swung it behind but failed to make contact with the creature's head. He watched in shock as blood ran down his legs and splattered on the floor.

"Fucking chop it off me!" he screamed, holding out the hatchet to Tara.

Coming to life, Tara grabbed the hatchet from Jeff with both hands. She swung it down hard toward the creature. At the same time, the creature tugged Jeff backwards, which sent the sharp hatchet blade deep into Jeff's shoulder. He screamed as she pulled it out and swung it down again, this time striking the creature hard in the back of its head. Green goo bubbled out from its wound as Tara kept striking its head.

Suddenly the creature released its hold on Jeff, letting out a high-pitched scream and shaking its head frantically, spraying Jeff's blood throughout the shack. As quickly as it had appeared, it retreated down the hole.

In stunned silence, Jeff turned and saw blood dripping down into the fishing hole. He kicked the hatch down then lay over it.

Tara stared down at him, her sweatshirt and arms covered in his blood. With the hatchet still in her hands she began to whimper at the sight of Jeff lying there in a pool of blood.

Jeff's body jerked as something pushed up on the small hatch door under him. *Could it be that same creature*, Tara thought, *or was it another one that picked up the scent of blood that dripped into the hole?*

The pounding got more intense as Jeff tried his best to keep his weight over the hatch door.

The hatchet shook in Tara's hands as she trembled. "Go away!" she screamed but the pounding continued.

Jeff felt weaker by the second, his vision became a black and white kaleidoscope, with things slowly turning white. *Is it snowing in here?* he thought.

Large tears ran down Tara's cheeks as she saw Jeff's eyes closing. "I can't let you die like this!"

Jeff's eyes went to the firewood box as he took his last breath.

## CHAPTER 46

A Carrie Underwood song played on the jukebox. Lori bent over the pool table, her long blonde hair brushing against the green felt as Kevin wrapped his arms around her.

"That's good. Now lower your head down just a little more for a better view. Now, are the balls lined up?"

Lori nodded.

"OK. Now gently take a few practice strokes and hit that first ball right in the middle."

Not a word was spoken from John or Janice who stood at the end of the table.

Lori hit the cue ball, which made contact with another ball, which hit another ball into the side pocket.

"Yes!" Lori hollered as she jumped with joy and high-fived Kevin.

John held up his beer for a toast. "To Lori's first combo!"

Janice glanced at John. "I hope she doesn't own a Louisville Slugger!"

Kevin smirked. "Hell, that's OK. I removed my headlights earlier."

They laughed at Kevin's comeback and toasted to Lori's combo.

"It sounds like you folks are having a good time," said a raspy voice from behind.

Old Charley had crept out from the dark kitchen with a mug in his hand.

Kevin smiled. "How are you doing this evening, sir?"

Charley groaned. "I'd feel a whole lot better if they'd open that trail and let them snowmobilers through, especially after that big dumping of snow."

Lori nodded. "Yeah, that's bullshit, closing the trail so the Army can practice for terrorists."

Janice smirked. "If they ever have any problems with freakin' terrorists, all they have to do is call in Jack Bauer!"

They all laughed at Janice's joke except Old Charley. "Who is this Jack Bauer?" he inquired.

Lori shook her head and smiled. "Oh, it's really Kiefer Sutherland. On this TV show, "24", he plays the part of Jack Bauer. He's a slick agent who works for an anti-terrorist organization called CTU."

Charley nodded. "Guess I must've missed it. Anyhow, Lori, I just wanted to let you know that I got a phone call from the Chamber of Commerce. There's gonna be a town hall meeting at seven tomorrow night. They're gonna have a meeting for all of us who are pissed over the snowmobile trail being closed."

Kevin's mind reeled back *Could it have something to do with their UFO discovery?* "It sounds to me like there is more to it than they're telling the media."

There was a brief silence. Kevin's comment took Lori by surprise. She glanced at Kevin. "I think you're right. Would you mind attending that meeting with me? Maybe you'll have some insight into some of that military bullshit they're trying to feed us...and if it gets too freakin' political, we can always visit Darren at the Riverside."

Kevin liked the idea. Maybe he would learn something that would help with their theories concerning whatever the hell it was under the lake. "Sounds good, I wouldn't miss it for the world."

The look on Old Charley's face was one of absolute delight. "Well thank you very much, Kevin. I don't know how to thank you."

"You just did. Don't forget Charley, I'm from a small town where we also have our share of small-town political bullshit. This is just another pile."

Charley glanced at Lori. "Bring a couple of rounds for our guests and cook them up some bar munchies if they get hungry later. I'm calling it a night."

Later that evening Kevin held Lori's beer while she stoked the fireplace. Lori glanced over at John and Janice bonding over a game of pool.

"Well, it looks like they hit it off OK."

Kevin grinned. "Yeah, considering he wanted nothing to do with a blind date from Blind River."

Suddenly something from outside caught Lori's eyes. She put her hands on Kevin's shoulders and kept his back to the window.

"Oh my god," she whispered.

"What is it?"

"There is something I want you to see but we have to put our coats on first and you have to promise me you won't peek."

Kevin nodded as Lori led him to the coat rack.

After bundling up, Lori covered his eyes with her mittened hand and wrapped her other arm snuggly around his waist as she led him outside.

Kevin felt the cold night air against his face. The packed snow squeaked under their boots as they slowly made their way across the deck.

"OK," Lori whispered. "You can look now." She removed her hand from his eyes.

Kevin was mesmerized by an array of long, greenish beams of light that danced in the starlit northern sky. "Oh my god. The Northern Lights! They're awesome!" He put his arms around Lori and looked deep into her eyes. "I have to take a photo for my screen saver to remember this beautiful moment with a beautiful woman."

Lori was taken by his words and gently exhaled. "I feel the same way about you."

A moment of silence passed between them. Kevin lowered his head and gently kissed her lips as the Northern Lights flickered above. He embraced her in his arms. "You don't need traffic lights to slow you down in these parts."

Lori gazed up at the Northern Lights. "That's for sure. They seem to come naturally."

# CHAPTER 47

The following morning was clear and frosty as two snowmobiles travelled side-by-side on the north end of Lake Matinenda.

The sleds came to a halt when two fishing huts could be seen in the distance.

Smoke trickled up from each hut's chimney.

It was the hut on the left, with a snowmobile parked alongside it, that got the attention of Elaine, a seasoned Conservation Officer familiar with the area. She raised her helmet visor and looked at her riding partner, young OPP Constable Yves Forget. "It's most likely a local cottager who doesn't know the area is closed."

Forget raised his visor. "You're probably right. After we check it out what do *ya* say we drop by the Lodge for toast and coffee with Old Charley?"

Elaine smiled. "I think you mean toast and coffee with Lori. I see the way you look at her."

Yves had no comeback. He knew she had him pegged.

Within a minute or two they had their sleds parked and were standing outside the hut. They could hear the sound of a rock song playing from within but no one came out to meet them.

Judging from the frost that covered the snowmobile, Yves knew it had been parked for some time.

"Hmmm…no registration numbers," Elaine mumbled as she checked out the shack.

"Maybe someone's having a nap," Yves said as he stepped towards the door. He knocked on the door and waited for a few seconds and then knocked a little harder. "Hello…anyone there?" he hollered over the sound of the stereo.

Elaine stepped in front of a small window and put her gloves up to the sides of her face to block out the sun's glare. Peering inside, she noticed a clear plastic bag of marijuana sitting on a table between two stainless steel martini glasses that were half-full, but she saw no one in the dark confines of the hut. "Uh Yves...I think you should take a look at this."

Yves stepped up alongside Elaine and peered in. He couldn't help but notice the bag and martinis. His mind was in a swirl as he looked back at the parked snowmobile. "Whoever owns that sled probably had too many martinis and hitched a ride with someone else. Elaine nodded in agreement as Yves quickly wrote down the snowmobile's make and registration numbers in his black book. "I'll take a quick look inside. Maybe I'll find more surprises."

Elaine watched Yves as he opened the shanty door and stepped inside. She heard a loud thud then a horrified scream.

Elaine drew her pistol from its holster and rushed to Yves' aid. When she stuck her head into the doorway she was stunned to see Yves struggling desperately to get himself off of a body that lay on the shanty floor. Elaine knew the look on Yves' face mirrored her own: that of absolute shock. Every time he tried to stand, his boots slipped on the blood-covered floor. He grabbed the edge of the table to steady himself and then slowly stood. He reached over and disconnected an alligator clip from a car battery to silence the stereo.

Elaine gasped and holstered her pistol as she gazed down at the bloody body. She felt a sudden drag in her gut and held back her breath to prevent from throwing up.

Yves could see she was having trouble stomaching all this. "Are you going to be OK?"

Elaine nodded then stepped into the shanty, squinting, as her eyes adjusted. She was sickened by the sight of all the blood. She drew a sharp breath. "Shoot! Is all that blood his?"

Yves frowned and pointed down soundlessly to a large gash on the young man's shoulder.

Elaine's face tightened when she saw the gore.

Their eyes roamed the shack, landing on two snowmobile suits and helmets, which hung on the wall and on a pair of blood-soaked jeans and a pair of boots that were scattered about on the floor.

Elaine frowned as she moved closer to the suits. She fingered one "Well, this looks like it belongs to a small woman, and I'm willing to bet that those jeans and boots belong to her as well.

Yves nodded as he compressed the transmitter button on his police radio to speak to dispatch. "Constable Forget to dispatch… come in." After no response, he tried adjusting the transmission frequency and called out again but that failed as well. He scowled. "Shit! Not this again!"

Elaine glanced over. "I'll see if I can get through on mine."

Yves returned a doubtful look. "Sure… go ahead."

Elaine compressed her transmitter button. "Officer Campbell to dispatch…come in." She tried again. "Officer Campbell to dispatch…come in."

Yves groaned. "Go figure…just when you need them the most. I knew I should have taken that freakin' satellite phone instead."

They were suddenly startled by a knock from inside the firewood box. They jerked back and drew their guns and pointed them at the box. Their hearts pounded.

Yves' eyes narrowed as he motioned to Elaine that he was going to lift the lid.

Elaine slowly nodded then shifted her focus back to the box.

With one hand, Yves slowly raised the lid. It was only a few inches open when they caught sight of a bloody axe head with a set of eyes peering back from behind it.

Yves flung the lid back and then grasped his pistol with both hands.

Elaine's eyes were bulging in horror, looking down her gun barrel at a young girl holding up a bloody hatchet. The girl was trembling, her petite body blood-covered, crammed low inside the firewood box. Dark streaks of eye shadow and mascara were running down her tear-dried face.

Yves peered into her bloodshot eyes. "It's OK. We're the police. Put it down."

She didn't respond to his request. Her pale lips began to move slightly. "They'll be back," she whispered as she continued to tremble.

Elaine glanced at Yves. "I think she's in shock.

"Put it down now!" Yves repeated. He sighed and holstered his gun. "OK Elaine. You're going to have to help me."

Elaine nodded.

He slowly leaned towards the girl. It was like a wolf studying his prey. *Does she intend to run or fight?*

"You're safe now," he whispered and then slowly reached for the hatchet while Elaine kept him covered. He grabbed the hatchet just above the girl's hands and gently pulled it away and placed it down in the far corner.

Elaine let out a sigh of relief as she holstered her gun.

"They'll be back." the girl muttered again.

Yves' eyes narrowed as he glanced up at Elaine and then back at the girl. "Who will be back?"

She paused then repeated, "They'll be back."

Elaine reached out and gently laid her hand on the young girl's shoulder. "It's OK. You'll be safe now."

Yves realized that time was of the essence and he had to act quickly. Since the hut was a crime scene, his protocol was to stay and keep it secure until help arrived. He also figured that the girl would require medical attention. Yves checked his watch. He looked over at Elaine. "Would you mind driving to the Lodge to use their phone?"

Elaine nodded. "I can't imagine it will take more than an hour to get some help."

Forget eyed the girl intensely as she sat trembling. "Could you help me get her out from there before you leave?"

"Jeez, how long has she been in here?"

A minute or so later they had her sitting on the box. Elaine helped her get her snow-suit on.

"I'm sorry Yves if you get shit for destroying evidence. But keeping her warm is the right thing to do."

Yves nodded. He wasn't about to argue with Elaine. The fact that she was a Conservation Officer only gave her the right to protect and care for wild animals but he didn't want to go there.

Elaine exhaled, trying to keep her cool, as she remembered the large gash on the young man's shoulder. She watched Yves handcuff one of the girl's wrists to a handle on the wood box.

Elaine had just started her snowmobile when Yves poked his head out the door and shouted, "Tell Sergeant Cook that we'll need the Forensic Identification Unit from the Soo. And give them that sled's registration number."

"Not a problem," Elaine shouted. "Just remember to offer that poor girl some hot chocolate from my thermos if she comes around later."

Yves sighed. "Don't worry. I have everything under control."

## CHAPTER 48

Later that morning, Greg and J.P. were just finishing setting their lines when Kevin and John pulled up on their sleds. Greg approached them with an ear-to-ear smile as his radio played in the shanty.

"Well, don't you two look all bright-eyed and bushy-tailed this morning!"

"I tink dat's because dey got der oil changed," J.P. joked.

John smirked at J.P.'s joke and then noticed two snowmobiles parked at the distant hut. The OPP sled, with its red light rising up in the back, stood out like a sore thumb. John sneered. "That's strange to see a cop travel alone."

Greg nodded. "Yeah, me and J.P. thought the same, and I hope the hell he doesn't cut into our hot toddy time."

John glanced at Kevin. "Wasn't that a Conservation Officer we met that was heading towards the Lodge on the other side of Graveyard Narrows?"

"Hell yeah, come to think of it he was traveling like a bat out of hell."

Greg smiled. "I think you mean 'she'. That must have been Elaine that you saw, but that's very unusual."

Kevin's eyes narrowed. "I'm sorry Greg but I don't quite follow ya."

Greg took a deep breath. "Well, if you got a chance to see Elaine's shoulder patch it would have read, 'MNR' in big letters."

John nodded. "Yeah, no shit, it stands for 'Ministry of Natural Resources'."

Greg shook his head. "No, out here it stands for, 'Must Not Rush'!"

The boys laughed at Greg's joke.

As Kevin shook his head, Greg reached over and patted him on the shoulder. "I'm glad you're a good sport. Come on in, the coffee should be ready."

The radio suddenly went buggy with the familiar deep dreary sound.

"I'll shut dat dere freakin ting off dere," said J.P. as he made his way into the hut.

Greg frowned. "Well at least we caught the news earlier."

"Anything interesting?" asked Kevin, putting on his coonskin hat.

"Na, same old, same old. Some big brass from Homeland Security will be speaking at a town hall meeting in Blind River tonight to explain their terrorist exercises. At the same time the mayor's shorts are in a knot over the snowmobile trail being closed."

Suddenly J.P. jumped out from the hut with a horrified look on his face.

Greg looked at J.P. trying to catch his breath. "What in the hell is wrong with you?"

J.P. looked confused. "After I shut off de radio I saw a small red light going tru da floor and de stove and when I went close, I saw dat it went tru de roof as well."

"I *gotta* see this," Greg said, striding toward the shanty, with Kevin and John on his heels.

As they entered they got a whiff of burnt coffee that lingered in the air.

Greg was halfway across the floor when he stopped dead in his tracks. "Holy shit!" he blurted aloud. Sure enough, there was a red beam of light that was impossible to miss. With a diameter the size of a pencil, it came up through the floor, passing through the stove and catching the edge of the coffee pot before it exited out through the roof.

Kevin and John gaped in silence at the red beam streaming up through the stove.

When Greg went to reach for the coffee pot, John jumped out and grabbed his arm. "NO!" he shouted. He reached down and took a piece of firewood from the box. Greg watched intently as John waved one end of the wood across the light beam, slicing it, like a hot knife through butter.

J.P.'s jaw dropped as he watched John slice a few more. He couldn't wrap his head around it, seeing a beam of light cut through the wood like a chainsaw and hit the floor like slices of frozen bread.

"Well looky here fellows," said Kevin peering down at the Aqua-Vu. "That red beam is shooting right up from the top of that craft down there."

In seconds, all four were gazing at the monitor. They were amazed. It was like nothing they'd ever seen before.

Kevin pushed a few more tabs on his laptop to replay the video back just a little more. His gaze hardened. "Well, I'll be a son of a bitch!"

John cocked his head. "What is it?"

"Check out the time in the top left corner. It's approximately the same time that the radio went buggy."

Greg's eyes narrowed. "Could that beam be some kind of radio transmission that they're sending out? "

John nodded. "Yeah, like some kind of S.O.S."

"Maybe dat's E.T. calling home?" J.P. muttered.

Greg gave a nervous chuckle at J.P.'s suggestion.

Kevin looked up. "I think he might have pegged it. It's like every time they transmit, the intensity of the transmission is so strong that it knocks the socks off all local wireless signals that operate on a lower frequency like radios, cell phones or even a GPS if it's close enough."

Greg frowned. "Yeah...or even a quarter inch steel plate woodstove."

The comment made Kevin's mind rewind. He quickly brought up his latest e-mail and recovered the one that his buddy had sent him from NORAD. Kevin's eyes widened. "Oh my god...check out the coordinates on that Air Canada passenger plane that got its wing sliced off a few nights ago."

"Don't tell me," said Greg.

Kevin nodded. "Fucking straight above us."

"Holy shit! Then that's got to be how Brutal Bruce and his sled got sliced in half!" said John.

"It makes sense to me," said Greg. "But I wonder what attracted that craft to his sled in the first place?"

Kevin shrugged. "Seeing it happened at night, it could have been his head light ...like that one guy on the tour group from Elliot Lake...or maybe the magnetic field produced by the engine's magneto?"

Greg shook his head. "And to think young Darren could have been the next contestant."

John looked at Kevin. "So what now?"

"Well, we can call Canada Immigration and ask them to define 'illegal alien'," Kevin smirked. "Or...keep this discovery under wraps until we know a little more about them."

Greg nodded. "I'm with you Kevin. What do you suggest we do next?"

"Turn that radio back on low volume. When the beam shuts off, I'd like to hear the station come back on."

Greg nodded. "Good thinking."

J.P. jumped up from his chair and quickly turned the radio back on.

Kevin grinned. "Thanks J.P. I'm gonna replay last night's video and see what your friends were up to."

# CHAPTER 49

That same morning, General Mackwood sipped on a coffee with his boots up on his desk, while speaking to his wife on speaker phone.

"Well that was nice of them sweetheart. The next time you're in church thank them for their prayers and let them know that the Lord is leading this special mission in Northern Ontario.

An abrupt knock on the General's door interrupted the conversation.

"I'm sorry, sweetheart but I'm going to have to let you go now," he said, as he hung up the phone and took his boots off the desk.

"Come in!" he ordered. Mackwood looked surprised when the Major opened the door. He looked down at his watch. "Well good morning Major. Have you completed your mission already?"

The Major's grim face betrayed his emotions. "Uh...we were just about to depart when we had a little glitch."

The General's eyes narrowed. "'Glitch'?"

The Major cleared his throat. "Uh...yes, sir. It was just like our fighter planes the other day. Just as our choppers were ready to depart we lost all radio communication with them and our ground support as well."

Mike rolled his eyes. "For god's sake Major, your exercise is a fucking no-brainer. All you had to do was have three Apaches fly over the top of that fishing shack to intimidate them and then have a couple of your officers drop by to tell them that the area is closed for Army exercises and pick their brains at the same time."

The Major acknowledged the light reprimand with a grim smile. "Yes sir...with this clear sky, getting good space telescope coverage won't be a problem and the men have compass coordinates. I just needed your permission to proceed but your phone line was busy for some time, sir."

Mike exhaled, trying to keep his cool. "Proceed, Major."

# CHAPTER 50

Greg set down a coffee beside Kevin's laptop as the red pencil beam continued to glow behind them. "I've got to warn you Kevin, it's just coffee this morning. I didn't 'Canadian-ize' it because I expect to get a visit from that cop next door."

Kevin took a swig. "It's not bad Greg…for being brewed in a saucepan."

Greg muttered. "I tell ya, if we ever get to communicate with them E.T.'s down there I'm gonna make freakin' sure they come clean on a new stainless steel coffee pot for this shack. That sucker cost me over fifty fuckin' dollars."

Kevin glanced up from his laptop. "OK, we have an incoming at 4:46 pm."

"Oh my god! Did you see that gash on the back of that *fucker's* head?' said John from the Aqua-Vu screen.

"Yeah," said Greg. "I saw a bit of it too."

Kevin looked at John. "I'm sorry but I'll have to rewind it again for a better look."

"I tink we are going to ave company!" hollered J.P. from outside the hut.

Kevin looked up in alarm through the window and saw three helicopters approaching them in the distance. He glanced back at the red beam exiting through the roof. His mind reeled back to the Air Canada incident and he knew he had to act fast to somehow divert them from flying into the beam.

John's eyes widened. He realized the danger the choppers were in as the deep, pulsating sound of their engines increased through the still, morning air.

With no time to explain, Kevin rushed out to his sled and pulled a flare gun and a handful of rounds from his knapsack.

The guys watched from the doorway as Kevin positioned himself in front of the shanty. He broke open the single shot action of the flare gun and quickly loaded a round. With both hands he pointed the barrel straight into the sky. He waited a second or two until the choppers were about the length of a football field away and then began to fire away. It was after he fired the fourth flare that the lead helicopter pilot decided it was too risky to fly through the array of flares and banked his helicopter steeply to the left as the others followed suit, narrowly missing the shanty. Kevin sighed dramatically and dropped down on one knee.

An amused grin crossed Greg's lips. "Boy, have you got horseshoes up your ass!"

Kevin acknowledged with a grim nod as he watched the helicopters fly off in the distance.

John hollered, "Holy shit! Those fucking Apaches were fully armed with rockets."

Kevin stood. "That tells me that we're in their face."

John looked skyward. "Do you mean we're being watched by space telescopes?"

Kevin nodded. "By parking the shanty directly above that UFO, their heat sensors were obstructed from tracking it."

"Oh my god," said John, his voice infused with intensity. "They can't track what they can't see. They probably suspect that we're terrorists trying to hide a weapon of mass destruction."

Kevin eyed John intensely. "They dispatched those Apaches just to see how we would react. I've got a gut feeling that we'll be getting a ground visit next. I think we should be spending a little more time outside checking our lines and drilling more holes to look more like fishermen."

Just then the radio came back on. Greg glanced over his shoulder and noticed that the beam had vanished. "Son of a bitch. It looks like Kevin was right."

Minutes later Kevin was reviewing on his laptop.

Greg's face tightened when he saw the large gash behind the creature's head. "Yikes! That's one hell of a battle scar on that sucker!"

"Yeah," scoffed John. "That fucker probably bumped into that transmitter beam, eh."

A grin grew on Kevin's face. "That's what happens when you try to cut into an alien's conversation!"

John rolled his eyes. "Did I just hear Kevin try to make a funny?"

J.P. frowned and pointed out the window. "I'm sorry, but I tink dat we are getting company again dere."

The guys looked out the window and saw two snowmobiles approaching. Each driver was dressed in full winter whites, each had a rifle strapped to his back.

Greg sighed. "So Kevin, what do you recommend we do now?"

"Well, if you and J.P. don't mind staying put for just a few minutes, John and I will try to break the ice with them."

Greg nodded back with a grin. "Sure, this should be interesting."

Kevin and John waited until the two soldiers had parked their sleds before exiting from the hut. The soldiers were stuck for words when they saw Kevin and John dressed like them.

"Good morning fellows!" said Kevin with a welcoming smile as he reached out his hand.

The soldiers studied Kevin and John closely as they stepped off their machines. The first soldier was short and stocky with dark skin. He removed his right glove, then reached out and shook Kevin's hand. "Good morning. I'm U.S. Army Sergeant Buckle and this is my partner Private McCarthy from Delta Force," he said in a sharp voice.

Kevin gripped the Sergeant's hand firmly as he looked him in the eye. "I'm U.S. Army Sergeant Stephenson and this is my partner Corporal Gordon from the Canadian Forces.

Sergeant Buckle was stunned. He nodded and held out his hand to John. "Pleased to meet you Corporal Gordon."

"And you," said John as he shook their hands.

Kevin met Sergeant Buckle's eyes. "So I understand that you fellows are on a training exercise with Homeland Security."

The Sergeant nodded. "Yes. It's to strengthen the preparedness of North America against terrorist attacks. These exercises are carefully planned and closely controlled to ensure NORAD's rapid response capability."

Kevin glanced over at John. "Huh, so what do you think? Should we get our asses back to North Bay to help with this exercise and take in the rest of this fishing trip at a later date?"

John's eyes narrowed. "Not! Our response time hasn't been quite up to par lately. We're still trying to recoup from tracking Santa last month."

Buckle grinned. "It sounds like you two are having a fun fishing trip."

Kevin eyed Sergeant Buckle's rifle. "Do they still have trouble with them M-16's jamming?"

"Na, not since they improved on the ammo. You seem to be quite familiar with it Sergeant Stephenson."

Kevin nodded. "Hell, I burnt out my share of them at Fort Irwin."

Buckle was impressed. "You trained at Fort Irwin in California?"

"Yeah, a little over three years ago."

Just then Greg and J.P. stepped out from the shanty.

Kevin grinned at Buckle. "These are my friends, Greg and J.P. They have a cottage at the west end of this lake and are up here fishing while their better halves are soaking up the sun in Jamaica."

The Sergeant and Private stepped forward and introduced themselves. "So I guess you are aware of the exercises that we will be conducting with North American Defense Command and Homeland Security?"

Greg looked at Buckle. "We just had a sample earlier with three of your choppers that almost took the roof off my fishing hut. We've been here the last three days and only caught a bit about your exercises on the radio in our hut. It was lucky we even heard that much with all that freakin' interference we've been having!"

Buckle casually gazed around the perimeter to give Greg a chance to cool off. His eyes narrowed when he caught sight of the OPP snowmobile parked at the distant hut. "How long has that officer been there?"

Kevin shrugged casually. "That's a good question. It was there when we first arrived over an hour ago.

Buckle anticipated there'd be a conflict when he tried to force Greg and J.P. to leave the area. His expression hardened as he addressed them. "I'm sorry, sir but I'm in a hell of a dilemma. With the exception of Sergeant Stephenson and Corporal Gordon, all civilians are to be evacuated from this area."

Kevin smelled trouble brewing and knew he had to act fast to prevent a confrontation. "Uhh, just a second Sergeant. This is hardly the moment to debate politics but I'm almost certain that if you explain the situation to your next in command that Corporal Gordon and I could be made responsible for Greg and J.P. and if we stay within a five-mile radius during your exercise there shouldn't be a problem.

Buckle looked uneasy. Kevin's comment had caught him off guard. There was a moment of silence as Buckle and the Private climbed onto their sleds. "You've got me in a real dilemma here, Stephenson. I suppose I could throw it by him but if he's not in favour you can expect to see us back."

Kevin gave Buckle a reassuring nod. "I'm sure you'll say the right thing.

As the soldiers drove off, Greg patted Kevin's back. "Thanks a lot for coming to our rescue."

Kevin grinned. "Are you kidding? I came to *their* rescue."

A confused look swept across Greg's face. "You came to *their* rescue??"

Kevin lowered his voice. Delta Force soldiers are trained killers...experts in SWAT operations, hostage rescues and terminating terrorist cells. But when they start fucking with ice-fishermen in Northern Ontario things could get really ugly!"

Kevin's joke brought hearty laughs and broad smiles as they made their way back to the hut.

J.P. stopped in his tracks and looked up at Greg. "When dat Sergeant said he was in a 'dil-lem-uh' what was dat?"

Greg grinned. "Oh, you mean '*dilemma*'! It means he's stuck in a hell of a situation.

# CHAPTER 51

Elaine sat alone in the Lodge dining room. She sipped on a coffee and gazed out a window at two blue jays perched on a feeder as thoughts of the young lady in the fishing hut played in her head.

"Can I top up your coffee?" asked Lori, approaching her table.

Elaine gave a gentle nod. "Sure, go ahead. I guess it'll be a while before the OPP show up."

Lori looked uneasy as she filled Elaine's cup. "I wasn't eavesdropping while you were on the phone but that fishing hut you were referring to wasn't Greg's by any chance?"

Elaine reached for a sugar packet and slowly shook her head. "No, it's a new one. Not far from his."

Lori exhaled a sigh of relief as a gleeful look spread over her face. "Oh yeah, the one with the two horny couples with the loud stereo."

Elaine's eyes locked on hers. "Do you know them?"

"No, but a friend of mine who's fishing with Greg and J.P. mentioned that they were from Elliot Lake. You probably saw him and his buddy heading out when you first arrived."

"Yeah, I saw their sleds on this side of the Graveyard Narrows. But Lori, why don't you sit down for a minute and tell me a little more about this friend of yours?"

Lori flushed as she sat down across from Elaine. "His name is Kevin. He's a sergeant in the U.S Army and is stationed at NORAD in North Bay."

Elaine's eyes narrowed. "Is he the one who put the run on Brutal Bruce?"

"You heard?"

Elaine scoffed. "Are you kidding? I personally know officers that were glad to hear that Bruce finally got a taste of his own medicine. Even my riding partner who is waiting at the hut was hoping to meet him."

"Well let him know that Kevin is fishing in the hut close to him."

Elaine nodded. "I'll have to make a point of visiting him myself."

Lori paused. Her eyes stared into Elaine's. "I just want you to know that it wasn't his macho fighting skills that turned me on. It's his personality and his honesty and consideration of others that I like."

Elaine smiled. "He sounds like quite a man."

"Yes. He's even taking some time out from his holiday to attend that town hall meeting tonight on behalf of this Lodge."

Elaine gave Lori a reassuring wink. "From the sounds of it you snagged yourself a real keeper!"

## CHAPTER 52

Minutes seemed like hours for Constable Forget as he waited for help to arrive. He looked across at the girl sitting on the wood box. She was still trembling and in obvious shock as she gazed down at the body. Speaking in a gentle tone, he held out Elaine's thermos to the girl.

"Would you care for some hot chocolate?"

The girl silently continued to gaze at the body.

Suddenly, a loud thud coming from under the shanty floor jolted the inert body.

Yves dropped the thermos, jerked back in his chair and drew his gun. He took a deep breath as he gripped his gun tightly with both hands.

Another loud thud came from under the floor. Again it jolted the body slightly to one side, enough for Yves to make out a crease of a fishing hole trap door. He glanced across at the girl as beads of sweat rolled down his forehead. "What is it?"

"They're back." she whispered.

## CHAPTER 53

Greg stood beside the table, topping off everyone's coffee. "I just can't believe how calm you and John are! I'm fucking freaked out! Here we are drinking coffee less than a hundred feet above a UFO with them freaky things swimming under our feet!"

John reached out his mug for Greg to fill. "It's probably because we see them almost every month on our radar scopes."

Greg raised his brows as he filled John's mug. "You see UFOs every month?"

Kevin let out a short chuckle. "Hell, We see UFOs enter and exit our atmosphere consistently without being recorded."

There was a short silence as Greg filled Kevin's mug. "So why aren't they recorded?"

"Because it's not in our job description," said Kevin.

Greg jerked his head back. "Excuse me?"

John defended. "That's right. The command doesn't monitor comets, meteorites or any other so-called 'natural' threats. Only since 9-11 has NORAD been monitoring airspace within North America. It's only man-made threats that might come from the skies like missiles, jets or spacecraft that concern us."

Greg raised his index finger. "Ahh. You *did* say jets or spacecrafts?"

John grinned. "But we don't record or report them. To record a UFO you're looking at a ton of paperwork. Kevin and I wrote off that UFO down there as bad data when we thought it was a meteor but we kept its coordinates. If NORAD had to monitor all other so-called 'natural' threats we wouldn't have time to properly monitor other suspicious aircraft."

"I'm sorry John, but I find it hard to believe that all this freaky shit is going on under our noses, and no one in power seems to care," muttered Greg.

John raised his eyebrows. "Well it's not *all* swept under the table, you know, Greg.

It's just not the most prudent thing to get into politically right now. There is a fair bit of skepticism out there, which, bottom line, affects voter decision-making. And there is so much that is not known, which, if we admitted it, could cause mass panic. But two years ago, Canada's former defence minister Paul Hellier, spoke at an expolitics symposium at the University of Toronto and said that UFOs were as real as the airplanes flying over our heads. Who knows? Maybe Lake Matinenda is the next 'Area 51'."

Kevin looked up from his laptop. "Just look how far man has come in the last hundred years. From the Wright brothers' first flight to our space shuttles, just imagine what another culture somewhere out there could do in just a thousand years? That's the reason we should expect the unexpected. We are dealing with beings down there that are much further advanced than us and up until now they have been benevolent."

J.P. looked down at Kevin and shrugged.

"What I meant J.P. is that up until now those aliens down there have not meant us any harm. We just accidentally got in the way of their transmission beam."

J.P. acknowledged Kevin with a nod.

"Having said that, I think we should do our best not to piss them off."

Greg pointed up to the radio as the local news came on.

Dead silence ensued as the anchor reported a rash of UFO sightings in the region.

In addition to this news, a local resident on Lake Duborne, James Rajotte, claimed to have taken pictures of UFOs on his digital camera and e-mailed them to CTV and CNN news.

Greg's eyes widened. "Oh my god. There is going to be shit to pay for now!"

"Do you know this fellow?" Kevin asked.

"Yes. He's as honest as the day is long."

Kevin stared back down at the UFO on his monitor. "Well fellows. It sounds like your SOS has been answered."

There was the sound of a helicopter approaching.

Greg glanced out the window and saw that a police helicopter was about to land close to the other shanty. "What the hell!?"

## CHAPTER 54

Yves looked up at the officer who was securing the girl to a seat in a helicopter. "Like I said, the only thing that came out of her mouth was, 'They will be back'."

"That's OK, Yves," said an elderly detective standing next to him on the lake. He gave a confident nod as he looked down at the black body bag strapped to the helicopter's strut. "It looks to me like a bad combination of alcohol and drugs."

The helicopter pilot gave a thumbs up and started the engine. "OK, sir. I shouldn't be more than an hour."

The detective nodded as he pulled a satchel from the helicopter. "Call me Jake. An hour should give me plenty of time."

A minute later Yves and the detective stood facing the shanty as their backs were hit with a stinging spray of granulated snow that had been kicked up by the helicopter.

"Shit. I'm not going to miss this part of the job when I retire," scoffed Jake as he tried to shake snow out from his collar.

"In all your years as a detective you must have had some interesting cases."

Jake set his satchel down on the ice. "Oh yeah, I had some real doozies all right!" He pointed to the snowmobile parked beside the shanty. "You want to hear something interesting? The numbers on that sled that Elaine called in to us are registered to Dr. Jessop in Elliot Lake."

Yves jaw dropped. "Shit, I hope that wasn't his son on that stretcher."

"Well, I heard that the doctor and his wife were away on a cruise. While the cat's away..." Jake reached into his satchel and pulled out a pair of white disposable coveralls and two sets of latex gloves.

Yves grinned as he watched Jake fight his way into the coveralls. "What the fuck is this? C.S.I. Lake Matinenda?"

Jake gave a small chuckle. "Yeah, the low-budget version." He handed Yves a pair of gloves.

Yves held up his blood-stained hands for Jake to see. "If that body had any kind of disease then I've got it too."

Jake rolled his eyes and handed Yves a resealable plastic bag. "The gloves are for collecting evidence."

Jake's attention was drawn to the sound of J.P. starting the power ice auger next door. He looked towards the other shack and saw J.P. and Greg setting new lines.

"There was a lot of traffic around that shack today," Yves muttered.

Jake nodded. "We'll have to pay them a visit later but first I'd like to collect a few souvenirs and see what was making that noise under the floor you mentioned earlier."

Yves was right on Jake's heels as they entered the shanty. He watched as Jake placed a piece of firewood in front of the door to keep it open.

"You see Yves. Unlike "C.S.I." on TV, we turn the lights ON instead of fumbling over evidence with a pen light!" Jake reached down and picked up the bloody hatchet in the corner. "I think this would pass as 'Exhibit A'," he said as he slipped it into a larger plastic bag. He glanced down at the stainless steel martini glasses and bag of marijuana on the table. "If you don't mind bagging them, I'm gonna take a peek under the floor." Yves had an eerie feeling as Jake got down on his knees and lifted the hatch. "Hmmm...looks like a regular fishing hole to me."

From Yves' angle, something shiny could be noticed under the hollow floor. "I see something under there to your right."

Jake reached down into his coveralls pulling out a small flashlight, then he lay down flat on the blood-stained floor.

Yves watched intently as Jake peered under the floor with his flashlight.

A smile grew on Jake's face as he reached under the floor and brought up a clear bottle and held it above the hole. "Well how do you like that? Mongoose vodka on the rocks! Young people today sure know how to party."

There was a blast of ice cold water that shot up from the fishing hole and hit their faces. Suddenly Jake's right arm was enveloped in the jaws of a hellish creature. He screamed frantically as its long, razor teeth imbedded deeper into his arm. The creature then jerked the arm from side-to-side, which sent the vodka bottle rolling across the floor.

As blood spattered the walls, Yves drew his gun and tried desperately to take aim at the moving target, fearing he would shoot Jake in the commotion.

"Shoot it! Shoot it! Fucking shoot it!" Jake screeched.

Yves stepped forward and put his gun barrel close to the creature's skull. The jerking motion from the creature slammed the gun against the side of the hatch. The impact loosened Yves grip and he watched helplessly as the gun fell from his hand and into the hole.

Jake reached out with his free hand and grabbed the bottle of vodka and began clubbing the creature's skull.

Deafening shots of rapid gunfire rang out behind Yves, followed by a loud, hellish scream from the creature as the bullets penetrated its skull. It quickly released Jake's arm and descended down the dark hole.

Jake slammed the hatch down tight.

"What the *fuck* was that?" shrieked Elaine.

Jake took a deep breath and looked up at Elaine as she holstered her gun. "That, my dear, was the 'phantom of the shanty'."

Yves squinted at the sight of Jake's blood dripping down his arm and quickly removed his belt and wrapped it above the wound as a tourniquet. "I don't know where you keep your fucking horseshoes, but that *thing* must have just missed your artery. This should do until we get you to the hospital."

Jake jerked his head back to face Yves and Elaine then slowly unscrewed the cap off the vodka bottle as beads of sweat rolled from his forehead. "Can we form a little covenant between us?"

Elaine and Yves looked momentarily confused.

Jake, still in shock, grinned and held up the bottle. "What happens at Lake Matinenda stays at Lake Matinenda."

Elaine nodded. "Sure, I think we could all use a shot of that."

## CHAPTER 55

Lori glanced over her shoulder as Kevin drove out of the parking lot. "Are you sure that you're comfortable back there John?"

"I'll be fine. The drive to town isn't that long."

"So, do you and Jan have plans for tonight?"

Kevin gave John a mischievous grin in his mirror. "I know that if *she* doesn't...*he* sure as hell does!"

Lori poked Kevin with her elbow. "You're a bad boy!"

John chuckled. "I think she's got you pegged buddy. Jan said that the North Bay Skyhawks are in town to play the Beavers. We might catch that hockey game and then drop by one of the bars for a few games of pool."

"It might be a good idea to pay Darren a visit at the Riverside just to keep him in the loop," said Kevin.

Lori gently squeezed Kevin's hand. "Oh I'm sure he already knows what went on at Lake Matinenda today, and then some. I still feel sorry for Elaine waiting all day for that forensic team to arrive from the Soo. She was really pissed off when they phoned her back and told her that a helicopter had been dispatched from Sudbury almost two hours earlier."

Kevin nodded. "I guess it was an awkward situation for the emergency services but when you factor in the long commute from the Soo and towing a stretcher sleigh through Graveyard Narrows, I think that a helicopter was the right call."

John nodded. "Well, we figured something was up when we saw that police snowmobile parked there for the best part of the day but it really freaked us out when they brought that body bag out from the shanty. As for that girl, she looked terrible. They had to carry her to the helicopter, eh?"

Kevin glanced up into his rearview mirror. "Is it me John, or was that other officer favouring his right arm when he exited from that shanty?"

"You're right. I was about to say the same thing. And Greg was sure he heard gunshots coming from that shanty when J.P. was running the ice auger."

There was a short silence and then Kevin gave a little chuckle.

"What's so funny?" Lori asked.

"Oh, it was something that Greg had told the officer that questioned us."

Lori sighed. "OK, let's have it."

"When the officer asked Greg if we had heard any loud screams or any other commotion coming from that shanty Greg told him that all we heard was Nickelback, and the screams that we *did* hear were the happy ones."

Lori grinned. "Oh my god, that sounds like Greg all right." She looked at Kevin. "When you mentioned earlier about finding it strange that the officer was favouring his right arm it reminded me of a strange story that I heard happened just yesterday on Lake Duborne."

Kevin glanced at Lori. "Are you talking about that UFO sighting?"

"Yes. How did you know?"

"We heard it on the radio," said John.

"Well, it just so happens that I went to high school with James Rajotte, the guy who took those pictures on his digital camera."

Kevin grinned. "You know, with the right software it's easy to do trick photography with a digital camera."

"I know that Kevin. But what makes James' pictures so authentic is that there is a provincial police officer standing beside his cruiser, in the background."

"Hmm...now that makes the story a little more interesting."

"Oh, believe me, it gets better," said Lori.

"It gets better?"

"Oh yeah. In James' photo, you can see that the officer was also taking a picture at the same time."

John felt sorry for Kevin, having to keep their secret from someone he cared for but he knew he had to play along. "Holy shit Lori, do you think that the officer will go public?"

Lori nodded. "Apparently he swore under oath."

They were just past the Riverside Tavern when Lori pointed. "You can drop John off across from that Sears Catalogue Depot."

John had only left the Jeep for a second when Kevin leaned toward Lori and gazed into her eyes. "I was going crazy thinking about you all day."

"Oh, me too." She leaned over and gave him a long, passionate kiss.

Kevin checked his lips in the mirror for lipstick.

Lori smiled. "Don't worry Kevin, I'm sure the whole town knows about us."

Kevin grinned. "Is Blind River *that* small?"

Lori nodded. "Oh yeah."

As Kevin's Jeep entered the Town Hall parking lot Lori was shocked to see that it was completely full. She couldn't help but notice CBC and CTV news vans parked close to the entrance.

Kevin shrugged. "So where do we park?"

Lori pointed. “Just up this street by the Court House.”

After Kevin parked the Jeep Lori smiled and pointed to his coonskin hat. “I think it should be warm enough inside!”

# CHAPTER 56

It was standing-room only when Lori and Kevin entered the Council chambers. Kevin received a lot of cold looks as they squeezed their way along the back wall. It suddenly hit him that it was his military winter-whites that were provoking them. *They probably think I'm one of the Homeland Security soldiers that are training in their playground, he thought.*

An anxious mood lingered in the air as Town Councilors chatted among themselves and television cameramen waited patiently. The OPP was in attendance, two officers standing by at the exits. Finally, two men entered from a side doorway and the volume in the chamber suddenly lowered with all eyes focused on the men.

Lori held her hand beside her mouth and whispered. "That's the mayor. His name is Ron Goodlin." Mayor Goodlin was a middle-aged man, sharply dressed, who seemed to exude warmth.

Kevin kept his eyes on the man walking beside the mayor. He was younger and wore a US Army Major's uniform. Kevin was surprised that Homeland Security would use a US Army Major for public relations.

Mayor Goodlin and the Major took their place on a raised platform at the front of the room. Before opening the meeting, the mayor told the crowd how taken he was by such a large attendance. He noted that he hoped that the representative from Homeland Security would explain what their exercises were all about and why their area had been chosen. He advised that after their guest was finished speaking the floor would be open for a question period. He then introduced the Major Curtis Kelly.

Major Kelly charmed the audience by telling them how beautiful their part of the country was and said he planned to return in the summer for a fishing trip and a round of golf with the mayor. He apologized for any inconvenience that the exercises may have caused. He quickly got into the meat and potatoes of post-911. He explained how NORAD, the North American Air Defense Command, and Homeland Security were working together to protect North America and prevent further terrorist attacks. The reason, he said, for choosing the area for the exercises was due to its geography, a combination of large lakes and rivers and that the Elliot Lake airport had no commercial flights to schedule around which made an ideal portable command centre for their fighter jets and helicopters to operate from.

The Major won over business owners in the audience by detailing how much money they were spending just on hotel accommodations and meals for their pilots, ground troops and technicians.

The Major's speech left a bad taste in Kevin's mouth. He was certain that they knew all about the spacecraft on the bottom of Lake Matinenda. He couldn't stand to see the way the Army was pulling the wool over the audience's eyes.

His mind cast back to his twelfth birthday…standing with his mother, at the side of his father's sick bed, which would eventually become his death bed. His father had pulled out a white plastic bag from under his covers and handed it to him.

*"Happy Birthday son…I'm sorry I didn't wrap it."*

*Kevin's eyes widened after he looked into the bag. "Is it alive?"*

*His father chuckled from deep in his chest. "Don't worry son, it's dead."*

*Kevin cautiously reached in and pulled out a coonskin hat. He smiled, ear to ear. "It sure looks like the one that raided our garden."*

*When he pulled it over his head his mother chuckled. "Our little Davy Crockett."*

*"Who's that?"*

*Kevin's father reached under his pillow, pulled out an old book and handed it to Kevin. "This book was given to me from your grandfather on* my *twelfth birthday."*

*Kevin held it out and read the title,* Tales of Davy Crockett.

*"I'm sure you'll enjoy it son. Davy Crockett stands for the spirit of the American frontier. He was a soldier, a trapper, an explorer and an expert marksman. He was remembered for helping people in need. Now son...would you mind opening it up and reading the top of the first page for your mom and dad?"*

*Kevin read. "'Be always sure you are right, and then go ahead.'"*

*His father reached down and patted his head. "Now never forget that."*

The first speaker to stand was from the Ontario Federation of Snowmobile clubs. His beef with the Major went on for a good twenty minutes and he covered how the closing of the trail had affected businesses that paid for advertising on trail signs and maps.

With a humble look, the Major apologized.

The next speaker stepped up. He was a young man who looked like he had a couple of drinks under his belt. He spoke about the countless hours he had spent volunteering, slashing out the trail that he used to take his children snowmobiling on. He said he felt robbed after investing thousands of dollars on a new snowmobile, insurance and trail pass. "Thanks to the *fucking* Army," he shouted, "My sled is parked in my backyard!"

The Mayor waved to the police to escort the man out.

People felt sorry for the young family man and called out to the Mayor to let him continue. Others in the audience booed the police as they escorted him out.

Kevin looked at Lori. "This is *bullshit*!" He made his way briskly to the microphone.

The room suddenly calmed as people stared in wonder. *What was a soldier doing at this meeting?*

The Major was shocked as Kevin stood at attention, in his US Army fatigues and saluted him. "Sergeant Kevin Stephenson from NORAD, North Bay, sir!"

"At ease!" the Major ordered.

"Good evening Mayor and Council," Kevin started. "Unlike Major Kelly, who is here on business, my buddy and I are enjoying a fishing trip up at Lake Matinenda, while staying at the Lodge. We've only been here a few days and the Major sure pegged it when saying how purdy this part of the country is. With all this great Northern hospitality, good fishing, fresh air and clean water, it's gonna be really hard to leave this beautiful place. Hell, you may have to escort our asses out of here."

The crowd laughed.

"One thing we did notice when we first arrived was the warm and friendly hospitality we received from people and businesses. The large turnout here shows me how tight-knit this community is and that you don't take kindly to being bullied by bureaucracy. It seems kind of strange to me that Homeland Security would move in without any notice and then try to justify themselves by telling you that it's the terrain that appeals to them. And an airport that has no commercial flights? Go figure? They probably think that you folks are mushrooms: they can keep you in the dark and feed a lot of ka-ka to you!"

The Major roared. "You're out of order, Sergeant!"

Kevin wasn't intimidated by Kelly's rank. He had never been surer of a decision: this was the time and place to educate the locals on what was really happening. He locked eyes with the Major. "Oh, and I suppose Homeland Security was in order when they moved in unannounced. I'm sure it would have been a "big" problem for Homeland Security to use one of those many provincial parks that are closed this time of year, or one of the Army's training grounds like Burwash, south of Sudbury, or Petawawa. And the need to use the Elliot Lake airport? The fact that our fighter aircraft cruise at over one thousand miles per hour means it wouldn't take a fighter aircraft long to engage in one of their exercises when deployed from the North Bay military base."

The Major was visibly sweating as most of the audience began to nod in agreement.

"The Major said that Homeland soldiers are staying and eating at hotels in Elliot Lake. These rooms would normally be booked with snowmobile tour groups anyways. Let's do the math. One soldier per day, for a room and meals is probably just over a hundred dollars times ten days is just over a grand. Hell, that young family man who was just escorted out of here spent over ten times that amount on his snowmobile alone! If I were you folks, I would be wondering why freaky things are happening around here lately. What about the constant radio signal interruptions or that Air Canada passenger jet that had its wing-tip mysteriously cut off? Now Homeland Security suddenly decides to cordon off this same area? What is *with* that?"

All eyes were now on Kevin as the Major sat stony-faced and silent.

"So are they really here on training exercises or are they here for another reason? Are they searching for that wing-tip...or something that's responsible for cutting it? Or maybe it's the same thing that is somehow interfering with radio signals? I strongly recommend that you folks get in their faces. Contact your local Provincial and Federal politicians and demand answers as to what is happening. As for me, I'm going back fishing for a few more days before I head back to work and a heap of 'taters to peel for expressing myself here this evening."

A man stood up in the front row and began to slowly clap his hands in appreciation for Kevin's speech. He was joined by others and then within seconds the whole room, including Mayor and Council, were applauding Kevin's speech.

# CHAPTER 57

As Kevin and Lori entered the Riverside Tavern people high-fived Kevin and thanked him for his speech.

"Now that's telling them!" shouted an attractive lady who looked to be in her late forties. She was sitting at a table with other women her age. They all stared hungrily at Kevin, their eyes traveling up and down his fit body.

Kevin graciously bowed his head. "Well thank you, mam."

Lori grabbed his hand and led him away.

Kevin couldn't believe how fast news traveled in town. "How in hell...?"

Before he could get the words out, Lori pointed to a big screen TV in the corner that was covering the town meeting.

Kevin rolled his eyes as he followed Lori to a pool table where John and Jan were playing a game. John was about to shoot the game ball. He looked up and raised his voice over the jukebox. "Don't even ask. We left after the first period. The Beavers were up three-zip and our Skyhawks really sucked. So...can I buy you two celebrities a beer?" John motioned to Darren to bring them a round.

"You really spoke well tonight," said Jan as she patted Kevin's hand.

Kevin flushed. "Well I didn't like to see that Major pull the wool over their eyes."

Lori rubbed Kevin's shoulders. "It was nice of you to do that."

Jan checked her watch and smirked. "I don't mean to pry Lori, but Kevin's speech ended about twenty minutes ago and it's only a two-minute drive from the town hall."

John grinned mischievously. "You should be asking Kevin that question."

Kevin didn't comment. He knew that not answering it would drive John crazy.

"We dropped by Action-Plus Video and rented a chick-flick," said Lori.

An amused grin crossed John's lips. "Oh yeah? Is that when two hot chicks are doing it?"

The girls exploded in laughter, defusing John's question instantly.

Jan glanced at John. "No ya dope, it's a romantic love story!"

John rolled his eyes. "Oh...for a second there I thought Lori and Kevin were like friends with benefits and were watching adult videos together."

Jan smiled. "You men really like to dream."

"You know what they say," John quipped. "When you stop dreaming, you stop living."

Darren set down a tray of beers. "It sounds like you guys are having fun."

John smiled. "Oh yeah, we're talking about chick-flicks."

"Is that when two chicks are...*you know*?"

Lori rolled her eyes. "Oh jeez, not you too!"

Jan took a swig of beer and looked at Lori playfully. "Thinking with the wrong head seems to be a guy-thing."

Lori smiled at Kevin. "Excuse me. I'll be right back."

Jan stood. "I'm right behind you, girl."

"What's up with them?" asked Darren as he unloaded his tray.

John grinned. "Ah, it's a girl-thing."

"So what's been going on at the hut since I've been away?"

Kevin took a swig from his bottle. "I guess having a laser beam pierce through your fishing hut from an alien vessel under the ice would kind of freak out most folks."

Darren's eyes widened. "Fuck *off*!"

John countered. "No shit. I wouldn't have believed it if I hadn't seen it myself. It even went through Greg's freakin' stove. We figure it's some kind of mega radio SOS signal that they're transmitting that's been fucking up radio signals and is responsible for slicing Brutal Bruce and that passenger jet's wing."

Kevin pulled out a business card that had been slipped to him by a TV reporter after his speech. He laid it on the table.

Darren looked at it. "Hmm...Gord Nicholls from CTV, he's the real deal, man."

"He seems to think that I know more than I'm telling."

"Are you going to let him cover the story?" asked Darren.

"I'm considering."

"A guy I know from high school dropped by here today to show me some very interesting photos."

"Let me guess," said Kevin. "A spaceship with a police officer and cruiser in the background?"

"You *fuckers*!" Darren scoffed. "You have better contacts at Matinenda!"

...Lori stood alongside Jan, in front of the washroom mirror, as she applied her lipstick. "With all this free time from the trail being closed, I wish I could spend a little of it with Kevin."

"Oh yeah, I'll take care of that. It's been too long since you've been with a man. You're going to have to get his interest in something other than fishing before he becomes prey for one of those cougars."

Lori giggled. "I guess you saw them at that table."

"No shit," said Jan. "I thought they were going to rape him! And you should have heard their comments when they saw him on TV. There's probably a pool of estrogen under their table!"

Lori rolled her eyes. "I can imagine."

"Well, you can't blame them. He showed himself to be intelligent, funny, and so damn easy to look at."

They made their way back to their table.

"Hey Darren, are you heading out to Matinenda in the morning?" asked Jan.

Darren nodded. "That's the plan."

Jan looked at John. "Well there's your ride back to the Lodge."

John glanced at Kevin.

Kevin shrugged. "Hell John, don't look at me. I'm not your mother."

"I have an extra helmet," said Darren.

John knew that Kevin must have read his mind. The timing was good. They could both have their time alone with the girls. "Sure Darren. What time do we leave?"

"Be at Tim Horton's for seven."

# CHAPTER 58

A romantic song played on the jukebox as Kevin and Lori exchanged lingering glances.

"I like a man who's willing to try different things." Lori raised her martini glass and clinked it gently against Kevin's and then took a sip.

He followed suit. "Hmm...not bad."

"A little different from your Jack Daniels, eh?"

Kevin looked down in his glass at a toothpick loaded with olives. "That's for sure, and it comes with an appetizer to boot!"

Lori laughed as she pushed the power button on the TV remote. "I'm sorry but I like extra olives in mine."

"Hell that's fine Lori. I kind of like 'em too."

Lori glanced down at her watch. "I wanted to catch the late news. You might be on it."

Kevin smirked as he raised his martini. "I'm sure they don't want to hear a redneck speak!"

Lori leaned over and gently stroked his hand as she peered into his eyes. "So, have you received any more e-mails from your mom lately?"

"I'm not sure. My laptop has been at Greg's hut for the last couple of days."

She thought he was being a little too trusting. "You don't think you're taking a chance leaving it there?"

"Are you kidding? With Homeland Security, NASA, and NORAD monitoring the hut, I know I can sleep sound."

She laughed. "It's nice that you have a good sense of humour."

Their laughter was broken by loud music from the TV, which signalled a breaking news story. Lori grabbed the remote and increased the volume. The anchorman was at his desk.

"*Our breaking news story this evening comes from Blind River . . .*"

Hairs rose on the back of Kevin's neck.

Photos of a UFO, like the one he had seen on the bottom of Lake Matinenda, lit up the screen.

*These startling photos you see were taken simultaneously north of Blind River by two local residents, James Rajotte and OPP constable Nick Foxwell. The photo on the left was taken by James Rajotte. It shows OPP constable Foxwell in the background of an alleged UFO, holding up his camera while standing next to his cruiser. The photo on the right was taken by constable Foxwell and it shows James Rajotte holding up his camera in the background of what appears to be the same UFO. This next clip was taken earlier this evening, at a town hall meeting in Blind River where discussions concerning the sudden closing of a provincial snowmobile trail by Homeland Security took place. There are allegations that the trail, which is in the same vicinity as the terrorist training exercises, is where strange occurrences have been taking place.*

*United States Sergeant Kevin Stephenson of NORAD, North Bay, questioned United States Major Curtis Kelly regarding an Air Canada passenger plane that had a large part of its wing cut off in the same proximity as the training exercises. Also discussed was the ongoing sporadic interference with radio transmissions. The town was left hanging when the Major refused to respond to the Sergeant's questions.*

Lori was startled by the ring of a phone. She answered it, her eyes glued to the set. "Good evening, the Lodge…" A grin grew on her face. "Yes Jan, we're watching it on CTV. You're *kidding*!?" Her jaw dropped. "The same story is on CNN? Oh my god! I'll call you back later!" She hung up. There was a moment of silence.

Kevin gave a grim nod. "I heard…and I am *so* history!"

Lori pressed the power button on the remote. "You were off-duty and there is something called freedom of speech."

Kevin took a large belt from his glass. "Right, try telling them that!"

Lori eyed him with uncertainty. "You were just trying to help people, where's the crime in that?"

Kevin exhaled. "Trust me, you don't play political hardball with the Major. That's a big time no-no, especially on CNN." He brought up his glass and gulped back the rest of his drink.

Lori grabbed his empty glass. Jan was right, Lori thought. She had been waiting too long and Kevin was the right man. She felt the urge to kiss him and didn't resist. She liked the warmth of his mouth and the sensation of his tongue. She forced herself to stop, knowing that Charley could enter at any time. She sat a loonie on the bar. "Why don't you play us a few more songs while I mix us up another?"

Kevin nodded with a grin as he got down from his stool.

"Oh, and can you pick C-22 for the last song to dance to? It's "Truly, Madly, Deeply," by Savage Garden.

# CHAPTER 59

General Mackwood was in a bitter rage as he spoke on his phone to the Vice-President. Major Kelly sat nervously waiting to address Mackwood next.

"Yes, I don't think we should waste any more time on this issue. The story about the meteorite emitting radiation sounds believable. Get it out to the press asap. Yes Scotty, Arrowhead is good to go. Sure...twenty-four hours works for me. Oh yeah, this will show them what they're playing with. Twenty-four hours will give me more than enough time to set the stage. All right then Scotty, I'll talk to you later. Bye for now."

Mackwood looked content as he hung up the phone. He looked across at the Major and shook his head. "You should have ordered him to stop."

"I'm sorry sir but he wasn't on duty and it was a public question period. If I had ordered him to stop, the smart-ass would have reminded me, in front of those TV cameras, about freedom of speech. I tell you sir; he had me by the balls."

Mackwood's eyes narrowed as he leaned over his desk. "You mean he played you like a violin. It's our turn to have home-field advantage now that he and his buddy are back on our turf. I want you to dispatch a chopper out there and get his ass back in this office asap."

The Major nodded eagerly. "Just him, sir?"

"Yes. His ass is property of the United States Army. He will cooperate."

"And if he doesn't?"

Mackwood paused for a few seconds and took a deep breath as he tapped his thumbs on the corners of his desk. "Should it come down to that, he's to be told that *Uncle Mike* wants to have a little chit-chat."

Kelly lowered his voice. "Did I hear you right, sir?"

Mackwood rolled his eyes as he took his seat. "That's right Major. I'm his uncle. He's my sister's only child. His dream was to serve his country as a Delta Force soldier. Less than two years ago he was one of our best soldiers that ever trained in SWAT operations, Hostage Rescue and Surprise Raids. He was hand-picked from the Combat Applications Camp at Fort Bragg by Major Thompson to be placed in his special operations command."

Kelly's eyes widened. "OK, I remember him now. So how in hell did a soldier of his caliber ever end up with his ass in a cushy job as a radar tracker with NORAD in Canada?"

Mackwood rubbed the back of his neck. "Kevin was about to be sent out on his first hostage rescue mission in the Middle East when my sister got wind of it. Kevin is her only child. She lost her husband ten years ago to cancer so Kevin is all she has left in her life. When Kevin first enlisted I gave her my word that he would never see combat. When she found out about Kevin's mission she thought she was going to lose her son and she had a nervous breakdown. She ended up being hospitalized."

"I'm sorry to hear that, sir."

"I tried to help by using my pull but now I'm caught in the middle of this bullshit. When I first found out from my wife that he was in the same area on a fishing trip I thought that perhaps we could get together and maybe patch things up. After finding out he was on Lake Matinenda I began to wonder if he had any connection to what was going on down there." Mackwood gave a chuckle. "We're talking about *aliens*. There's no way he or his friends could be communicating with that spaceship down there. But I'm sure when we get his ass in here; he'll tell us why they moved that shanty above it."

# CHAPTER 60

The radio played in the shanty as Greg and J.P. stepped out to greet the boys. Greg glanced at Kevin and started to laugh. "According to the news, you sure showed the Major where the bear shit in the buck-wheat!"

Kevin smiled at Greg as he put on his coonskin hat. "Hell, I just wanted to set him straight on all that there grief they caused y'all."

Darren nodded. "Oh yeah, I think you pissed him off big-time! When John and I dropped by Tim Horton's earlier there were at least half a dozen army trucks in the parking lot."

Kevin shrugged and looked at John in bewilderment.

"He's right," said John, as he unfastened his helmet strap. I was going to tell you."

"Let's take it inside," said Greg.

The packed snow crunched beneath their boots as they made their way towards the shanty.

They chatted over breakfast while Kevin replayed the Aqua-Vu. They became silent when the local news came over the radio.

*Moose FM Radio has just been informed that Homeland Security has discovered a meteorite that has crashed in the area where they are training. Unlike other meteorites, this one is emitting high levels of radiation. They are concerned for the public's health and have called for an immediate evacuation in the areas just north of Blind River on Highway 555, starting north of Lake Duborne. Northshore Radio will be giving hourly updates as public service announcements. In other news, a spokesman for Transport Canada stated that it was this same meteorite, or a part of it, that was likely the cause of the mishap with the Air Canada passenger plane just days ago, in the same area.*

Greg gasped. "Where in the hell are they getting these stories from? Aren't the writers on *strike* in Hollywood?"

Kevin looked up from his laptop. "I reckon they just found themselves another way to skin a cat, and that would explain them there army trucks in Blind River."

J.P. bent his head sideways and raised his index finger. "I tink I 'ear one of dem dere 'elicopters."

Darren's eyes widened as he peered through the window. "Holy shit, he's right!"

They watched intently through the small shanty window as a fully armed Apache helicopter landed within seventy yards from their shanty. A soldier stepped out and made his way toward them.

Greg glanced at Kevin. "I'm sure it's that same Delta Force Sergeant from yesterday."

Kevin closed his laptop and made his way to the door. "Yeah, I get the feeling the Major is still a little pissed with me and expects an apology."

All eyes shifted towards the open doorway when the Sergeant appeared.

"Well, if it isn't Sergeant Buckle," said Kevin, smiling. "What brings you by on this fine morning?"

The Sergeant ignored Kevin and poked his head into the shanty as though he were doing a body count. "Well, don't you guys look all warm and cozy?"

Greg held up his coffee mug. "Care for a fresh one Sergeant?"

"No thanks. Maybe some other time sir. I'm on escort duty this morning." He paused and then looked at Kevin with a big smirk. "You have a Fan Club at our Control Centre that is dying to meet you. I think one of them is Uncle Mike."

Kevin grinned. Buckle had caught him totally off-guard. "Sounds to me like I pushed a wrong button over there."

The guys remained speechless and watched Kevin as he took his last mouthful of coffee and then pulled his coonskin hat down tight around his head. "Keep the coffee warm. I don't expect to be long." He looked confident as he left the shanty.

Greg glanced at John. "Who is this 'Uncle Mike'?"

John frowned. "Damned if I know."

They gazed out the window at Kevin, hunched over and shielding his face with his mitt from the sharp ice granules that were being kicked up from the helicopter blades. The tail on his coonskin hat flapped frantically in the wind as he neared the helicopter. As soon as Kevin and Buckle were seated, the chopper lifted off and banked hard to the left and then headed eastward.

# CHAPTER 61

As the helicopter approached the airport, Kevin couldn't help but notice six F-16 Fighter Falcon jets and three Apache helicopters sitting ready to be deployed at a moment's notice. He glanced sideways at Buckle.

"You sure got some big-time firepower down there."

Buckle nodded back with a confident smile. "You got that right. Three of those Falcons will be used by our western Air Defense sector this Sunday to secure the airspace over the Superbowl."

After they landed, Buckle wasted no time getting Kevin to the General's office. Kevin knew they were close when he caught the familiar odor of cigars lingering in the hallway. He removed his hat when Buckle knocked on the General's door.

"Come in!" said a raspy voice.

They were quick to salute the General when they entered. Mackwood scowled from behind his desk. "You're dismissed Buckle!"

As the door closed behind Buckle, Mackwood indicated a chair in front of his desk for Kevin to sit on. He chuckled. "So, you got your ten minutes of fame? Did the Mayor give you the keys to his town? What in *hell* were you thinking?"

Kevin tried to counter as he sat down but couldn't get a word in edgewise.

"You carried on like some kind of radical from the sixties!"

Kevin sighed dramatically. "I'm sorry, sir but I just couldn't take any more bull from that Major."

Mackwood rolled his eyes. "Oh for heaven's sake Kevin. To harbour a weapon of mass destruction and then suddenly be concerned for people is absolutely ludicrous!"

Kevin was stunned by his uncle's harsh remark. He shook his head and spoke as calmly as possible. "Believe me sir. We parked that shanty over it by accident. And who's to say it's a weapon of mass destruction?"

Mackwood held up his hands. "You said so last night when you mentioned the Air Canada passenger jet that had its wing cut off in the same area. And I've got to hand it to you. It was a hell of a slick move when you used that fishing shanty to shield that craft under the ice. I'm just curious why you didn't mention that snowmobile that was sliced in half?"

Kevin sighed. "I said that it was a mystery how that plane had its wing cut off in the same area that you cordoned off. And now I'm sure that I have the answer to that, as well as what was causing all those radio and electronic interruptions."

The General had no interest in what Kevin said. He just frowned and shook his head. "I'm sorry, Kevin but the only logical conclusion I can draw from this is that there is an ungodly thing on the bottom of that lake and whatever planet that it's from, it means us harm. And you can rest assured that I'll have it extracted before the media can get their hands on another alien story. God knows we don't need another Roswell incident."

Kevin remembered his mother's e-mail comment that his uncle would receive a big bonus at the end of this mission. He realized that his opinion meant absolutely nothing.

The meeting was suddenly interrupted by frantic knocking on the door.

"Come in!" Mackwood ordered.

Major Kelly entered and made his way briskly towards Mackwood's desk without acknowledging Kevin. "I'm sorry, sir but we have ourselves a little problem."

"Go ahead and speak freely," said the General as he glanced across at Kevin. "He knows everything."

Curtis continued. "It looks like we have a political situation."

"What do you mean '*a political situation*'?" Mackwood scowled.

"We just found out from the local Provincial Member's office that a good part of the area in which we are evacuating is owned by Indians from the Mississauga First Nation Reserve."

"Hell," scoffed Mackwood. "We don't discriminate. We'll evacuate them too."

The Major lowered his voice. "The problem is notifying their Chief. It appears she is in transit up north and can't be reached until later today. She would have to sit with her council before she could proceed with an emergency plan."

Mackwood pounded his desk. "Son of a bitch! That could take another forty-eight hours."

The Major stared down at Kevin. "And after the Sergeant's performance on TV last night, they just might have second thoughts on leaving their land."

Kevin saw his opening for a foothold and took it. He cocked his head up at Major Kelly. "Are you kidding? That idea with the meteorite is great. Especially when the locals find out that I'm working for you."

Mackwood's demeanor changed instantly and he broke into a broad smile. "If this is your idea of a joke you're walking on pretty thin ice."

Kevin frowned. "Well after last night's 'performance' I reckon it would be good for the locals to know I'm in favour of what you are proposing. My involvement would help bring credibility to your meteorite find. And from what I heard on the news about a rash of UFO sightings it sure as hell sounds to me like E.T.'s buddies are searching for him."

A moment of silence passed between the men. Mackwood put on his reading glasses and gazed down at a sheet of paper on his desk. "I understand you put in for a transfer to NORAD's main technical facility at Cheyenne Mountain Operations Centre in Colorado?"

"Yes sir, I applied for that posting last month."

Mackwood peered over his glasses with a mischievous glint in his eye. "If you and your friend are willing to work with us I can have you transferred there with a letter of recommendation, but if you feel that there are personal issues from our past that might cloud your judgment I want you to bow out now, and return to North Bay."

Kevin knew he would have to make some concessions if he chose to collaborate but he also knew that he could utilize this time to his advantage. A smile grew on his face. He held out his hand to his uncle. "You can count on us sir."

Mackwood's face brightened. "You *ain't* seen *nothin'* yet," he said reaching out his hand.

After going over the details, Mackwood accompanied Kevin across the tarmac to a heavily guarded hanger. He motioned to a soldier to unlock its doors. "What I am about to show you rules in air superiority."

Kevin was stunned into silence as the doors opened. He gazed at the sleek black arrowhead-shaped plane that glistened in the sun's rays which streamed through the open doors.

Mackwood glanced at Kevin with his chin held high. "So what do you think?"

"Oh yeah, I'm *very* impressed, sir. But I don't see a cockpit for the pilot."

"That, my boy, is Project Arrowhead, the world's first space plane. It has no cockpit because it is pilotless. It's computer-controlled by satellites. It can fly at supersonic speeds just outside the earth's atmosphere. Its weaponry consists of a high-tech laser beam that is capable of taking out six targets at once."

Kevin smiled. "Or some sort of invasive craft under the ice?"

Mackwood patted Kevin's shoulder and winked. "I know you'll do a terrific job."

## CHAPTER 62

As Kevin stepped down from the chopper, Buckle gave him a thumbs-up. "It's great to have you on the team!"

Kevin returned a stern nod and then turned his back as the chopper lifted from the lake. As he watched the helicopter disappear over the tree line he wondered how he was going to break the news to his friends.

"Well hello, stranger!" said a familiar voice from behind. When he turned around he was surprised to see Lori standing in front of the shanty with a welcoming smile. He flushed with an ear-to-ear smile as he trudged through the snow.

"How in god's name?" Before he could finish speaking, Lori pointed to a vintage snowmobile parked alongside the shanty.

"Charley calls it 'Old Betsy'. It doesn't look like much but it gets you there."

Kevin put his arms around her waist and gave her a welcoming hug followed by a long kiss.

"O.K. you two. That's enough! Your coffees are getting cold and we're dying to hear a story," said Greg from the doorway.

Lori gazed into Kevin's eyes. "Don't worry. They told me everything."

Kevin sighed. "I'm sorry. I just hope you're not upset with me."

"Are you kidding? If I hadn't seen it for myself I would have thought you were on drugs!"

"Hell, if you think this is bizarre just wait til I tell ya'll what's gonna happen. You're gonna think I was on drugs!" Kevin's news caught them totally off-guard.

Greg glared disapprovingly. "Pardon my language Lori but *fuck* that bullshit! I'm sorry the General is your uncle and all but I'll be goddamned if I'm *gonna* move this shack so he can demolish a crippled spacecraft and who knows what kind of chemicals might be onboard the craft and emitted into this lake. Not to mention a possible rebellion from those other UFOs that have been spotted in the area when they find out that we terminated their buddies. What the hell is he thinking?"

"I'm sorry," said Lori. "But I have to agree with Greg."

The expressions from the others spoke for themselves.

"I was hoping you folks were all on the same page," said Kevin.

"So what's in it for you?" Greg probed.

"Nothing too exciting, just a transfer to NORAD's main technical facility at Cheyenne Mountain in Colorado, with a letter of recommendation."

"Fuck *off*!" John gasped. "That's the posting that you put in for last month!"

Lori looked up, confused. "So does this mean you'll be leaving?"

Kevin grabbed her hand and stared into her eyes. "Only if you good people don't want my help."

"What! You're not worried about pissing off the General?" asked Darren.

Kevin shrugged. "What's he gonna do?" Go ballistic? Before my father died, he told me as long as I lived to never forget a quote from a famous American: 'Be always sure you are right, and then go ahead.' Well I sure as hell believe it's right to take a stand against nuking that spacecraft and I'm ready to go ahead and do my best to prevent it."

John leaned over the table and patted Kevin's shoulder. "You can count me in."

Darren nodded in unison. "I believe you two are a blessing in disguise — I'll help you any way I can."

"I'm sure grateful to your father for raising such a fine son," said Greg. "So what famous American was that quote from?"

Kevin tapped the side of his coonskin hat. "Davy Crockett."

"If I had to pick a man to fill Crockett's shoes, you'd be the one," said Greg. "So what's the plan?"

Kevin looked down at his watch. "My uncle expects me to keep in contact with him three times daily by cell or Lodge phone. My first job was supposed to be to relocate this fishing shanty so the enemy spy-satellites could watch that ungodly thing down there."

"He called them 'ungodly'?" asked Darren.

Greg rolled his eyes. "Someone should tell him to read the bible where it mentions that God created the universe!"

"I guess he wants to terminate one of God's creations," chuckled Darren.

"Go figure. It sounds like a big-time propaganda stunt to intimidate the Chinese with that high-tech space plane."

"So what's our window on relocating this shanty?" asked Darren.

"Not yet," Kevin groaned. "The General is waiting for the Chief of the Mississauga Reserve to get back to him. He freaked when he found out that she had to sit down with her Counsel before she would proceed with an emergency plan."

Greg laughed. "We heard about it on the news earlier. I know for sure that our MPP wants a better relationship with Native communities and in the back of his mind he must be remembering the showdown in Oka, Quebec. He'll make damn well sure that Homeland Security communicates with the Chief before any evacuation takes place to avoid a freaking blockade on the Trans-Canada."

Kevin arched his brows. "That should help us buy a little more time to work on a plan."

Lori glanced down at her mug and noticed that her coffee was rippling. "What the hell?" she muttered.

The rippling increased as they all stared down at their mugs in awe.

Darkness suddenly poured in from outside. The shanty had been overcome by a dark shadow from above. The hut began to vibrate with a deep pulsating sound.

J.P. jerked his head back and gazed out the window. His eyes widened when they made contact with a large, circular, metallic object. "Oh my God!" he hollered frantically. "It's one of dem!"

Greg jolted backwards when he noticed a red beam. It pierced through the floor and the stove as it had before and made another hole through his coffee pot and roof.

Lori closed her eyes and trembled. "God help us!"

Kevin took her hand to comfort her. No one moved.

Suddenly everything stopped. It was as if someone had turned off a light switch somewhere.

Lori slowly opened her eyes and took a deep breath. Kevin wrapped his arms around her shoulders and gently embraced her. "You OK?" he whispered.

She looked uneasy but nodded. "I'll be fine."

John chuckled nervously. "I think they made contact."

Still traumatized, Greg glanced over at his coffee pot leaking onto the stove. He deeply inhaled and exhaled a couple of times.

Kevin smiled. "Those aliens sure have a way of bringing out the Darth Vader in you!"

"He does dat a lot when he watches dem Toronto Maple Leafs play hockey!" J.P. joked.

Greg reached down for his bottle of rum and sighed. "I expect better company with Captain Morgan."

# CHAPTER 63

Kevin was following everyone as they made their way into Greg's cottage, when his cell phone rang. He took the call on the porch. After a brief conversation with his uncle he entered the cottage. All eyes were on him as he removed his parka.

"Was that the General?" asked Greg as he stoked the stove.

"It sure was. He told me that they watched our episode on their control monitors from NASA's space telescopes. Apparently that saucer came out from nowhere and ground control was surprised that we didn't bail out."

John felt something was wrong in Kevin's mannerism. "Let me guess. The General is adamant about getting that hut out from there?"

Greg scoffed on his way to the fridge. "Pardon my language again, Lori, but if he expects me to move it now, he can suck my ass."

Darren chuckled. "Well I guess he got the word!"

Kevin was careful in answering John's question. "Yes, he was hoping we would move it this afternoon but I told him maybe tomorrow morning."

"That's if he's lucky," said Greg as he made his way to the table with his hands full of beers. "First we'll need a few cold ones to give us ideas on how to deal with those poor aliens frozen beneath."

John grinned. "Now you're talking my language."

As Greg handed Kevin his third beer he noticed that he was deep in concentration. "So do you have a plan for us yet? Or do you need a few more?"

Lori looked at her watch and smiled. "I think the plan is to get back to the Lodge."

Kevin gazed up at Greg. "You mentioned about coming up with an idea on how to deal with those aliens stranded under the ice?"

Greg slowly nodded. "Yes I said they were frozen beneath."

Lori glanced at Kevin with her hands apart. "So where are you going with this?"

Kevin chuckled, which got everyone's attention. "Earlier today my uncle told me that I was walking on very thin ice; well where would I have to travel to on Matinenda to find thin ice?"

Darren's eyes widened. "Oh my god! Lure them to Graveyard Narrows!"

"Good move," said Greg. "But how would that be possible? First you would need to cut a hole the size of this cottage on unsafe ice and then lure that space craft under it...and who's to say that it would fly out afterwards?"

John chuckled. "Well, we got the hole in the ice licked."

Greg looked confused. "You're losing me."

"Kevin is an explosives expert."

"You boys have explosives?

"Enough to sink a battleship. I had intensive explosives training with Delta Force," explained Kevin. "I only needed a little bit from our armoury to get a sample from that so-called meteorite but I somehow ended up with a case in my Jeep."

"OK," Greg nodded. "I get ya. So you're gonna blast a hole at Graveyard Narrows to free the saucer but then how would you attract them there? By telling them that we have free beer and pizza?"

Kevin took a sip of beer and glanced at Darren. "You have a pretty fast sled?"

Darren chuckled nervously. "*Fuck* that. One close call is enough for me. If you have a death wish then go ahead."

Kevin broke out in laughter. "That's not what I was thinking. I have a gut feeling that spacecraft is attracted to light at night and that's why it followed you, Brutal Bruce, and that tour group at night. We know that Bruce was sliced in half with their laser only when they transmitted. I wonder if we could rig some bright lights to a sleigh and then tow it with a long rope to Graveyard Narrows."

Greg gave a supportive nod. "I think we have the technology. I have an old sleigh in the woodshed that we can fasten a few sets of floodlights to. We can put my generator in the back of a snowmobile and then run an extension cord to the tow-rope back to the lights. I don't want that goddamned laser beam destroying any more of my things."

Darren raised his bottle. "To an awesome plan!"

After they toasted, Lori noticed an odd look on Kevin's face. "Is there something wrong?"

"Ah shit!" said Kevin. "I almost forgot that Delta Force has six snowmobiles that are on patrol, twenty-four-seven."

"Then we'll just have to create some kind of diversion," said Greg.

Kevin retrieved his laptop and set it on the table. "Do you guys know roughly where those UFO pictures on Lake Duborne were taken?"

Lori glanced over at Darren. "Wasn't it close to Battle Point?"

"Yeah," said Darren. "In that little bay in front of Mrs. Stiller's place."

"Does she live there all year-round?" asked Kevin.

Darren nodded. "Oh yeah, my buddy Jake plows her driveway."

There was a long pause as Kevin opened his laptop.

Greg stood from the table and pointed his index finger up. "Thinking about that sleigh in the woodshed gave me an idea, but first I have to visit the little house at the back."

Kevin gazed at his monitor. "I'm really curious to see where this Battle Point is."

Lori slid a business card over to Kevin. "I meant to give you this at the fishing hut. He dropped by the Lodge this morning just after you left. He said you could call him twenty-four-seven on his cell. He thinks you have a story."

Kevin glanced down at the card. *Gord Nicholls, CTV News*. "Hmm...He's persistent isn't he? This could be our ticket to participate publicly."

Minutes later Greg re-entered the cottage with a bulging green garbage bag. "When Darren mentioned Mrs. Stiller's place, I couldn't resist. I've got sixty feet of rope lighting with a hundred foot extension cord in this bag. I figured that if we doubled it and then laid it just under the snow about a hundred feet out on the lake in front of Mrs. Stiller's place that it would make for an entertaining event!"

Lori shook her head. "You're so bad!"

"It also comes with a timer and a variable lighting adjuster. We can set it to glow from dim-to-bright for special effects. All we have to do is pre-set the time and plug the extension cord into her boathouse and then we're good to go!"

Kevin let out a playful gasp. "OK Greg, I'm sold! But how can we be sure she'll be looking towards the lake?"

"Are you kidding?" Greg laughed. "With all the hype about UFOs I would phone to tell her that we had one on this lake and advise her to keep an eye out. Believe me Kevin, when it comes to keeping secrets on Lake Duborne, Mrs. Stiller is known as the leakiest boat."

"OK, it's up," said Lori gazing at the monitor.

Darren pointed to the top of the screen. "That's Mrs. Stiller's place right there."

"What's this?" said Kevin as he pointed to a line that crossed an inlet on Lake Duborne.

"Oh, that's the high-voltage hydro line," said Greg, now looking over Kevin's shoulder. "It runs along with the gas pipeline just north of us and then heads east towards Elliot Lake. Sledders use that land route early and late in the snowmobile season to avoid dangerous ice conditions on the lakes."

Kevin nodded. "Can it be accessed from this end of this lake?"

Greg glanced across at J.P. "Can you bring up a map of this end of the lake?"

With a tap from Kevin's finger, the map was up on the screen. Greg reached over Kevin's shoulder and pointed to a long inlet at the north end of Lake Matinenda.

Kevin studied it for a few seconds and then glanced up at Greg with a puzzled look. "I don't get it. That looks like *this* location."

Greg grinned. "It is. We have an old trail that starts right behind the woodshed. It will take you to that hydro line in seven minutes. We only use it for hunting or if the ice conditions are bad."

An amused grin crossed John's lips. "Screw NORAD, Kevin should apply to the Pentagon as a strategist and operations advisor! Check it out! That good ol' boy knows full well that NASA's heat sensors can't track us under those high voltage power lines."

Kevin nodded, his grin wide. "And remember to turn your lights out so they can't get a visual from their space telescopes."

Greg chuckled. "It should be fun trying to follow that trail in the dark."

Kevin went to his backpack and returned to the table with two sets of weird looking goggles. "This is where these night-vision goggles will come in." Kevin's cell phone rang. He glanced down at the caller i.d. "It's the General."

The room fell silent as he took the call.

A few minutes later Kevin folded his phone. He looked uneasy.

Lori lowered her voice. "Is everything OK?"

Kevin shrugged. "Our window just got smaller."

Lori's jaw dropped. "Did they get the word from the Chief to evacuate?"

Kevin heaved a sigh. "Yes. And he expects the shanty to be moved by ten A.M. tomorrow. He'll be nuking that craft twenty-four hours later."

Greg lowered his voice. "You mean he

wants us to set the stage so he can strut his new toy?"

Kevin grinned as he gazed down at the newsman's card on the table. "NOT! We're setting the stage for *ourselves*."

## CHAPTER 64

The morning sun was cresting over the snow-covered pines as Kevin and John returned to Greg's cottage.

Greg's eyes widened as Kevin exposed a sleigh full of army gear. "Holy shit! When you said you needed J.P.'s sleigh to bring a few things over I thought you meant explosives."

John reached into the sleigh and pulled out two sleeping bags. "All this stuff is for your cottage. It's the least we can do for providing all those great meals and brews, not to mention your great hospitality."

Greg shook his head. "No freaking way. I can't take this from you guys. You're risking your jobs and lives for the fate of this lake and people and god knows what else."

Kevin grabbed a sleeping bag from John and tossed it at Greg. "Ah then just look at it as a return on your tax dollars."

Greg glanced down at the bag as he caught it and smiled. "Well, now that you put it that way . . ."

J.P. pointed down at a large green box. "I tink I know what's in dat dere."

Kevin reached down and lifted the lid. "I knew you guys were curious to see what I was going to use to punch that hole."

Greg and J.P.'s eyes brightened as they gazed down at six explosives. Each were form-fitted into foam.

Kevin reached down and pulled one out.

Greg grinned. "Those grey things look like freaking beehives."

"That's exactly what we call them," said Kevin. "I'll be hooking them up in a series on the ice. The concussion will open a hole big enough to go trolling in."

They watched Kevin intently as he went back to the sleigh and pulled out a small box, the size of a deck of cards, with a button on top.

"This is the wireless remote. It's capable of detonating those beehives from up to a mile away. After I drive through the Narrows, John will compress this button and blast the opening behind me and, god willing, free that spacecraft. I just hope that those E.T.s will find favour with our light show we're gonna prepare for them."

"Oh, I'm pretty sure we won't have any problem coaxing that spacecraft off the bottom," said Greg with a confident smile.

Kevin gazed at Greg with wonder as he repacked the explosives. "Don't tell me you two paid them a visit last night?"

Greg looked guilty. "We had that sleigh rigged up shortly after you guys left and after a few more brews we decided to test her."

"So was it successful?" Kevin asked anxiously.

"Oh yeah, big time. We only had the lights on for a few seconds and that craft shot up like a bat out of hell." Greg chuckled. "My little bitch here almost shit his pants when they turned on their bright lights under the ice."

J.P. scoffed. "I don't tink dat's funny, me."

John grinned. "I can imagine how Darren felt when that bright light under the ice followed him."

Kevin glanced down at his watch. "Darren and Lori should have left the Lodge by now. I'm just curious how Darren made out setting up those lights at Mrs. Stiller's last night." He paused as he looked towards the lake. "I think I hear their sleds coming."

Greg looked uneasy. "Or maybe it's a couple of those Delta Force soldiers on patrol. Quick, go ahead Kevin and park that sleigh in the woodshed next to the other one while we stand guard."

To Kevin's relief, a few minutes later Greg walked around back with Darren and Lori to join Kevin in the woodshed. Darren chuckled when he saw floodlights fastened around the outside of the sleigh. "You got that sucker looking like a Christmas tree."

Kevin glanced at Darren. "So, how did it go on Lake Duborne last night?"

"We're good to go and I set the timer for eight P.M. and as for those night-vision goggles, they're fantastic! I had no trouble following that power line."

Greg nodded. "That's great. I'll phone Mrs. Stiller around ten to."

Darren glanced up at Greg. "So where are we towing your fishing hut to?"

Greg smiled. "I thought that maybe we could take up position just to the left of Graveyard Narrows, and then we'd have box seats for the showdown."

# CHAPTER 65

Tension hung in the air as the group patiently waited for the General to call.

Greg glanced at Kevin as he stoked the stove. "So did you and John have any problem setting the explosives?"

"There was one real thin spot where we placed one of them so we pushed it out a little further out with a long pole."

John gave Kevin a reassuring nod. "Well, I was really impressed with your work."

Lori exhaled silently as she squeezed Kevin's hand. "I'll be so glad when this is over."

Kevin's phone finally rang. The room went silent.

"Hello."

*Pause*

"No sir. We had no sightings around here."

*Pause.*

"No sir. We're *gonna* pack it in shortly."

*Pause.*

"You're welcome sir, and God bless you too."

A big grin grew on Kevin's face as he folded his phone. "Well, the General saw us relocate this hut from the space telescope and they took the bait—hook, line and sinker. He said that he was gonna head back to his hotel room."

Darren breathed a sigh of relief. "Thank god. I was worried that I didn't set those lights right."

Kevin chuckled. "Are you kidding? The Major just dispatched his patrol unit to Lake Duborne to check out some kind of mysterious craft."

Greg glanced at Lori. "See, Mrs. Stiller didn't have a heart attack. It was the way I spoke to her."

Lori rolled her eyes. "Oh yeah, I can imagine!"

John looked uneasy. "So I guess this means it's showtime."

Kevin nodded and handed John the detonator and his digital camera. “I heard that a picture is worth a thousand words. You’ll be in the best position after you blast that hole.”

Lori pulled out a camcorder from her jacket. “Between the two of us I’m sure we’ll have some awesome shots to email Gord Nicholls for the evening news.”

Kevin took his last sip of coffee and headed out of the shanty, with Lori at his side. As he stepped out onto the lake he gazed up at the starlit sky. Lori leaned towards him and didn’t hesitate to express her feelings. She hugged and kissed him in front of his friends.

Kevin didn’t mind. It reminded him of his mother doing the same thing to his father before he would leave to work in the dangerous coal mine.

“I’m sure glad you’re using my snowmobile,” said Darren. “With its long, wide track and speed you won’t have to fear any open water, eh.”

Kevin glanced down at his watch then climbed onto Darren’s snowmobile. “Well, let’s git ‘er done.”

Greg raised his mug to Kevin. "Here's to ya good buddy. Hey, I'll have one Canadi-anized for ya when you get back!"

Kevin smiled back at Greg as he started the sled. Hell, I won't say no to that. God knows I'll need one!"

J.P., eyes wet, walked up to Kevin and patted him on the back. "I want you to know dere dat I tank god for you."

Kevin was moved. "Don't worry J.P. This will all be over before you know it."

Greg reached down and flicked the power switch on the generator. It started instantly and projected a bright light onto the lake. "You're good to go," he said as he patted Kevin's back.

Lori threw Kevin a kiss as he drove off.

"Well I better get in position," said John as he started his sled.

# CHAPTER 66

Back at the General's office, Mackwood and Kelly were in the midst of a pre-victory drink when they received an emergency call to report immediately to the control centre.

"What seems to be the problem?" barked Mackwood as he and Major Kelly stormed into the control room.

A young technician shrugged and pointed to a monitor that showed a bright light that was heading north across the lake. Mackwood's eyes studied it closely. "What in god's name is that?" he muttered.

The technician glanced up. "It first started on the south end of the lake at the shanty that Sergeant Stephenson moved to those Narrows and is heading due north to where that craft is lying."

Mike took a deep breath. He picked up the phone and dialed Kevin. "I'll find out what the hell is going on." Mackwood's eyes narrowed when he got Kevin's voicemail. He slammed down the phone. "Damn you!" he muttered. "If he thinks he's got me over a barrel, he's got another thing coming!"

# CHAPTER 67

Kevin eased off on the throttle as he approached the north end of the lake. His headlight easily caught the bright orange ribbon that Greg had tied to a stick where the shanty had been previously parked.

He had just turned the snowmobile and almost had it in position when an enormous beam of light shot up from under the ice.

Even though Kevin was prepared for something like this, it made his heart pound. He squeezed the throttle down and followed his trail back. Looking in his mirror, he saw the light from the spacecraft following close behind the sleigh. All he could do was hope that he could continue on like this to Graveyard Narrows.

J.P.'s eyes widened as he spotted a bright light approaching in the distance. "I tink dat's him," he muttered.

Every second seemed like an eternity and their minds whirled while the group stood outside the small shack, waiting for Kevin's return.

John could also see the bright light from his high, rocky position along the Narrows, patiently waiting for his time to push the detonator.

Kevin was halfway across the lake when a bright light completely illuminated the night sky from behind the sleigh like a baseball stadium. When Kevin looked into his mirror, he was shocked to see that another spacecraft, like the one that had hovered over the shanty, was following about a hundred feet above the lake.

Suddenly, the familiar red laser beam from the spacecraft below pierced through the ice and made contact with the craft above. A loud explosion came from Graveyard Narrows, so loud that Kevin heard it over the sound of the snowmobile. He realized with dismay that the spacecraft's laser transmission beam signal had caused the wireless remote to pre-detonate the explosives.

Everyone watched in horror as they saw Kevin approach the dark, open water of the Narrows.

Lori lunged forward to flag him down but Darren grabbed her arm and jerked her back. "He's gonna make it," he said, staring into her eyes.

Lori shook her head frantically. "But the Narrows is wide open," she cried.

Darren gave her a reassuring nod. "My sled can handle that. Just get your camera out and start filming."

John knew he couldn't do anything to help from his position except take pictures.

As Kevin approached the Narrows he saw Lori filming him with her camcorder as Darren gave him the thumbs-up. J.P and Greg watched in awe.

With the bright lights from the spacecraft above, Kevin could easily see the black, open water ahead. He remembered what Darren had said about his sled's capability of running open water. He held on tight and kept the throttle pinned as the sled hit the open water. To his surprise the snowmobile kept steady and moved ahead as water sprayed out from the sides of the skis with a rooster tail shooting up from behind. He could see good ice less than fifty yards ahead and felt confident he could make it.

After what seemed like an eternity, Kevin felt the snowmobile take a hard jolt as it hit the solid ice. He drove far enough onto sound ice before stopping to make sure that the sleigh he was towing was in the centre of the open hole.

After killing his engine, he turned around and was surprised to see that the sleigh had come to rest on top of the spacecraft. The bright floodlights from the sleigh deflected off the spacecraft's metallic surface as it began to rise from the water.

He jumped from the snowmobile and turned off the generator then yanked on the tow rope, sending the sleigh sliding down the spacecraft and plunging into the lake below.

Kevin's breathing slowed and his eyes widened as he watched the two craft hover up alongside each other at about two hundred feet and remain motionless. Suddenly he caught a glimpse of Arrowhead as it circled the two spaceships.

Back at ground control, Mackwood knew that his space plane was now the centre of attention on enemy spy satellites. He gloated at the two spaceships that hovered side by side on his monitor. "That was nice of Kevin to put those targets on an equal playing field," Mackwood smirked as he pushed the "FIRE" button.

Kevin gasped when he saw two bright red laser beams shoot out from Arrowhead and strike each spacecraft. After thirty seconds or so of intense firing, the crafts remained hovering. Arrowhead's lasers seemed to have had no effect on them.

Back at ground control a technician lowered his voice. "I'm sorry sir but Arrowhead is maxed-out."

Mackwood flushed, mortified as he slowly released the button. He stared at the monitor in stunned silence, the two spacecrafts still hovering.

The group on the lake gasped as they watched one of the spaceships fire out a bright blue beam at Arrowhead, igniting a huge red fireball explosion in the sky. As the air cleared, the group watched the two spacecrafts hover off into space.

The General was devastated after realizing that his prize fighter had been terminated.

# CHAPTER 68

Three days later Greg and J.P. were fishing out on the ice at their original location.

"It's too bad dat Kevin and John can't make it to de fishing derby next mont'," J.P. muttered.

Greg took a sip from his mug. "Yeah... but I'm glad he got that position at the Pentagon. I wonder what impressed the President the most: the pictures from NASA's space telescope or the ones that Lori and John took?"

"Ya, I'm sure dat Kevin will do good for his country over dere," said J.P. as he made his way to the shanty.

"You can cut me another piece of that kielbasa," said Greg.

Seconds later J.P. poked his head out the doorway. "I don't see it, me!" he shouted.

Greg set his fishing rod down and made his way to the shack. "Are you blind?" he called back. "It's on the table beside the block of cheese."

J.P. saw nothing on the table. He glanced down at the open ice-fishing hole in the floor and saw a piece of brown wrapping paper swirling in the water.

Greg entered and noticed that the roll of kielbasa and the block of cheese were gone.

There was a stunned look on J.P.'s face.

"What's wrong?" asked Greg reluctantly.

J.P. pointed down at the hole. "I tink we got us a dil-lem-uh..."

Photo courtesy of
Westmount Photography

## Brian Horeck

Brian Horeck is the best-selling author of *Minnow Trap*. He was born and raised in Sudbury, Ontario and has lived in Blind River and Elliot Lake. Brian loves spending his free time hunting and fishing in the great outdoors of Northern Ontario.

Visit the author's websites at:
**www.frozenbeneath.ca**
**www.brianhoreck.ca**